A CRY IN THE NIGHT

Hillary was getting ready for bed when the phone rang. "Hello?"

The hesitation, the uneven, heavy breathing, knifed at her.

"Hello? Please . . . who is this?" she asked.

A little girl's voice.

"The bad man . . ."

Hillary forced herself to be calm, but it was the sensation of having a gun pointed at her forehead. She shut her eyes tightly and said, "Please, who's calling?"

"The bad man . . . the bad man I pretended killed someone."

Hillary couldn't breathe.

She couldn't think.

She gritted her teeth and felt her heart swing up and beat hard in her throat.

The voice again.

"Help me."

"I will. Please, tell me who you are. Tell me where you are, and I'll help you. I promise I will."

"The bad man I pretended killed someone. The bad man . . ."

"Please," Hillary whispered.

"The bad man I pretended killed someone . . . and he's going to kill again."

BOOK YOUR PLACE ON OUR WEBSITE AND MAKE THE READING CONNECTION!

We've created a customized website just for our very special readers, where you can get the inside scoop on everything that's going on with Zebra, Pinnacle and Kensington books.

When you come online, you'll have the exciting opportunity to:

- View covers of upcoming books

- Read sample chapters

- Learn about our future publishing schedule (listed by publication month *and author*)

- Find out when your favorite authors will be visiting a city near you

- Search for and order backlist books from our online catalog

- Check out author bios and background information

- Send e-mail to your favorite authors

- Meet the Kensington staff online

- Join us in weekly chats with authors, readers and other guests

- Get writing guidelines

- AND MUCH MORE!

**Visit our website at
http://www.pinnaclebooks.com**

JUST PRETEND

J. V. Lewton

PINNACLE BOOKS
KENSINGTON PUBLISHING CORP.

www.pinnaclebooks.com

PINNACLE BOOKS are published by

Kensington Publishing Corp.
850 Third Avenue
New York, NY 10022

First Printing: August, 1994
First Pinnacle Printing: September, 2000

Printed in the United States of America
10 9 8 7 6 5 4 3 2

One

It was a little girl's voice.

If you had been close to the phone booth in the parking lot of the Quik Shoppe which hugged the shore of Foxpath Lake on that early summer morning, you could have heard singing. A child's lyric or perhaps a nursery rhyme.

Inside the phone booth, a hand trembled as it held the receiver. In the other hand, small fingers pinched a quarter. The caller, badly frightened, had memorized a phone number and had to interrupt the plaintive lyric or rhyme to recite that number.

Beyond the phone booth, someone had stopped near the door of the Quik Shoppe to buy a newspaper from one of the newspaper dispensers. And beyond the Quik Shoppe, a mist hovered over the silken silence of Foxpath Lake. It was June, a warm Saturday, and so peaceful that terror seemed out of place.

But the would-be caller in the phone booth continued to tremble, breath catching, heart pounding. For a few moments, the singing started up again, the voice innocent. It had the tenor of someone whistling in the dark or walking through a graveyard. Then it suddenly ceased.

"I pretended a bad man . . ." the caller whispered into the receiver.

Pain flared. Fear clutched at the caller's throat like

hands threatening to strangle. And shadows, winged shadows, materialized, swarming menacingly about the phone booth like birds or huge insects. They slapped against the glass of the booth with a soft, wet sound.

"Help me. I pretended a bad man and . . ."

But the caller lacked the courage to drop the quarter into the coin slot and dial the number, and so the words went unheard. Darkness rushed through the caller's thoughts like a flooding river.

"I pretended a bad man and he's . . ."

Out on Foxpath Lake, up through the mist, the shadow of a child rose and seemed to echo the frightened caller.

"I pretended a bad man and he's . . ."

It was a little girl's voice.

"The vampires are coming! The vampires are coming!"

Molly Brannon stabbed a finger toward the door of her hospital room, her dark eyes wide with feigned fear, no smile on her extremely pale face.

Her older brother, Clay, turned as the "Heme Team"—a trio of hematologists, two men and one woman—entered the room in their white coats, carrying clipboards, smiling plastic smiles. Clay quickly reached for his hospital mask and tied it in place.

"Love your new wig, Molly," said the woman.

"Made it myself," said Molly, raising her hands weakly to adjust the Afro wig, and Clay noticed that several new tubes were running into the frail girl's IV. "Don't you think I look like Jimi Hendrix?" Molly added.

"Who?" said the woman.

Molly screwed up her face at Clay, and he smiled.

"You mean you don't know Hendrix?" Molly followed her question by pointing at a poster on the opposite wall. Below the words "They All Shine On" were pen and ink drawings of three rock 'n roll legends: guitarist Jimi Hendrix, Beatle John Lennon, and lead singer of The Doors, Jim Morrison.

The woman shrugged apologetically.

"Well, all I can say is that I like this wig better than the one you made of feathers and dyed pink."

The two male hematologists chuckled nervously, and then the threesome went about their routine examination of Molly's chart and of Molly herself, tapping and pressing at her, scanning her features as if she were a frog being dissected in a biology lab. They worked methodically, asking the usual questions; Clay could see how over the past fourteen months his sister had become intolerant of such examinations. He couldn't blame her.

"Hey," Molly smirked when the hematologists had stepped away in a knot, "aren't you vampires gonna suck out some more of my blood? I might have a cup or two left."

"No," they chorused. "We'll check on you again tomorrow."

"Tomorrow? What makes you think I'll make it past sundown?"

"Molly, don't!" Clay exclaimed through the mask.

"Tell 'em to go back to their coffins. I hope somebody stakes 'em in the heart," said Molly, pulling the regulation hospital sheet over her head.

When the hematologists had left the room, Clay removed his mask and dropped his face into his hands. He was sixteen. His sister Molly was eight, though Clay often felt that she was mature way beyond her years. Their relationship had always been close. They liked many of the same things: Foxpath Lake, Milk Duds, monkey boots, old rock 'n roll music—and virtually anything from the 1960s. Both of them wore a single earring bearing the shape of the peace symbol.

Clay loved his sister. And she worshipped him.

But Molly had leukemia.

She was a spunky, very bright little girl.

And she was dying.

When Molly let the sheet slip down from her face and saw Clay's bowed head, she gritted her teeth and said, "Darn you, Cab, don't do the sad music bit on me. Bradley's in charge of all the morbid stuff around here. And take off that silly mask. You look like you're fixing to rob a bank."

Whenever angered at him, or whenever she wanted to punctuate a serious comment, she called him "Cab," short for Clay Andrew Brannon, his full name. Bradley, a few years older than Molly, was one of her fellow "leukies" in the cancer ward. The mask was a hospital regulation for visitors. So was washing hands and wearing a paper gown and paper slippers.

Clay untied the mask and searched for a smile.

"Sorry. I think I'm just tired, you know. I did the famous Kroger's clean-up shift last night—we finished about 2:00."

Molly nodded and sighed; her eyes were droopy, as if the conversation were sapping her energy. To Clay, her emaciated body looked to have about as much substance as the paper gown he was wearing over his street clothes.

"How's Mom?" she asked.

"Same ole, same ole," he said. "She'll probably be up to see you sometime soon."

"Yeah, I bet she's got it on her calendar: 'Tomorrow, visit daughter at the morgue.' "

"Hey, who's being morbid now? You never know, she might make it by this morning."

But Clay and Molly both knew that Dora Brannon would not come; she had stopped visiting on a regular basis over a month ago because the stress of seeing her daughter in a near-death condition had become too much. In all likelihood, she would wait to be called for only one more visit. Not a visit, but a good-bye.

"Would you hold my hand," said Molly. "I'm gonna rest a little while before 'Just Pretend' comes on—it's on at 9:00, right?"

"Yeah."

Clay hesitated. Hospital regulations did not permit him to touch her, but since no nurses were around, he reached out. Molly's hand weighed barely more than a wadded up piece of notebook paper.

The touch of her hand sent waves of sadness through him.

"You want anything else?" he asked.

"Maybe you could put on some Joplin," she whispered.

"You got it."

He slipped a tape of Janis Joplin, Molly's favorite classic rock singer, into his boom box and kept the volume low. Molly closed her eyes when Joplin's barbed-wire voice launched into a song. Clay involuntarily squeezed his sister's hand, and for a score of moments he received vivid imagery of Molly in the months and years before leukemia stormed her body—images of a red-haired ball of energy swimming in Foxpath Lake and planning one day to be a great actress.

How different from the hapless creature he now gazed upon.

He thought of how much pain and discomfort she had endured in just over a year; most of it she had faced with a bravery he deeply admired. He had made every effort to be there for her every step of the way: the trips to the oncology clinic, the remissions and relapses, the excruciating bone marrow procedures, the hair loss as a side effect of radiation and cytoxan, the appetite stimulation and mood swing experience of Prednisone, the nosebleeds, the Petechiae or black-and-blue marks from skin trauma, the revolving door array of doctors and nurses, and the grim reality of being near other leukies.

"Molly?" he whispered.

She was asleep. The tilt of her head had caused her wig to slide to one side. Clay removed the wig and leaned down and kissed her bald head. His eyes teared. But then he swiped at them because he didn't want Molly to wake and see him that way.

Molly Ann Brannon hated tears.

He stared at the network of veins on one side of her head, and he listened to her shallow breathing, but it was difficult to detect it over Joplin.

"Molly, my precious Queen Mab, sweet dreams."

Pushing away from her bed, he settled into a chair, checked the time, and then opened a small, spiral notebook he took everywhere with him. Though it was nearly filled with his jottings, Clay always opened it to the very first page—to the inscription which read, "To a Great Writer from a Great Little Sister!" It was signed, "Molly."

Clutching the notebook, he received photographic images of the moment two years ago when his sister, a smile spreading across her face like sunrise, proudly offered it to him as a gift.

Yes, he wanted someday to be a writer.

It was his dream.

As he thumbed ahead to the page where he had started a new writing project, the morning nurse bustled in to check Molly's IV, gave Clay a cursory smile, and gestured for him to put his mask back on. He nodded that he would. When she left, he studied Molly's intensely pale face for a few seconds and then turned to a blank page of the notebook. At the top of the page he wrote a title: "The Girl Who Sailed Away."

It was to be a rehearsal story. A rehearsal of the inevitable. He vowed that this would be one entry he would not share with Molly. Too personal.

He wrote the first line: "This is a story about the girl who sailed away on a sea no one else had ever sailed." He liked the line. It was the beginning of a real-life fairy tale. And yet. And yet, how could this fairy tale possibly have a happy ending?

When he looked up from the page, he felt an electric shock run up both arms. It was Molly. She was so still. So very still it appeared that . . .

Clay lurched out of his chair and lowered his face close to Molly's. Panic wrapped around him, squeezing him like some massive serpent. She didn't seem to be breathing.

Molly, no, Molly.

Not this, Molly. No. Please, no.

He gently shook at her shoulder.

And relief coursed through him when her eyes popped open.

"Geez an' sneeze," Molly exclaimed, "why you waking me up? Joplin had rocked me to sleep, and here you are pawing at me. It isn't time for our show, is it?"

Clay smiled and shook his head.

"No, not yet. Sorry I woke you. For a second there I couldn't tell whether you . . . I thought that—"

"Thought I'd checked out, huh?"

She giggled.

And Clay felt silly.

Suddenly some words stuck in his throat: *I love you, Molly. Can't imagine life without you. I just can't.* Instead of those words, he said, "You know, the night nurse has been complaining about all your posters."

He swept an arm toward the nearest wall where half a dozen posters, mostly in psychedelic designs—"Flower Power" and "Age of Aquarius" motifs—jangled. They spoke of the 1960s human thirst for simple lunacy.

"Let her complain. She's a cow. She's mean as a snake. You like my posters, don't you?"

"Sure. But . . . it's not the posters, Molly. I talked to Dr. Winston this morning, and he says you're not cooperating with the treatment he's prescribed. Now, how are you gonna get better if you—"

"I'm not," said Molly. She spit out the words as if they tasted bad. *"That's* the point, Cab. Get real. There's a jillion tiny sharks in my blood, and they're eatin' and eatin' away—and nobody, not Dr. Winston or nobody else—can stop 'em."

The silence was heavy.

Clay intertwined his fingers. He had passed the point

at which he could offer Molly platitudes about getting well. And she had passed the point at which she could accept them.

"Can I get you anything?" he asked.

For a heartbeat or two, Molly's eyes twinkled.

"Yeah. Yeah, I know just what I want."

She gestured toward a lampstand atop of which rested a clock radio and a framed photo of her and Clay, a photo from the days of her flaming red hair and Clay's successful attempt at letting his black hair grow long.

Clay rolled his eyes.

"Your chocolate cache, right?"

She nodded happily, almost vigorously.

"Should be a brand-new box of Duds in there," she said.

But there wasn't. The top drawer of the lampstand was empty. No Milk Duds. No Snickers bars. No chocolate pecan clusters. Clay shrugged, and Molly's eyes shot sparks.

"Darn a'mighty," she said, her small mouth drawing up in a firm line, "who went and cleaned me out?"

"Any suspects?"

Molly thought a moment.

"Yeah. Lots of 'em. Probably one of the leukies."

And she reeled off several names: Robin, Craig, Drew, Bradley, Tanya—kids on the ward who weren't yet sick enough to be constantly bedridden.

"If it's another leukie, that's a real bummer."

No sooner had Clay spoken those words than he saw something in Molly's expression he didn't like—a mischievous light, a crooked smile.

"You could tell me, Clay. Wouldn't take hardly nothing for you to find out."

He knew what she meant.

He thrust his palm out as if to physically fend off her request. "No-o-o. Oh, no. I'm not doing *that*. No way. You know how much I hate—"

"Please," she interrupted. "We can't let a chocolate thief go running free."

That face.

Clay could fight it, but in the end he knew he would give in to that face. He knew he would do anything he possibly could for Molly . . . including the exercise of a peculiar wild talent he possessed.

When Clay was six or seven, doctors diagnosed it as "eidetic imaging"—the rare capacity for extremely vivid mental images, almost photographically exact, but, according to accepted scientific view, unreal. They claimed that Clay had no paranormal ability, just an unusually overactive imaging mechanism.

They were wrong.

And yet, because the exercise of his mental power had negative side effects—headaches, nausea, a painful roaring in his ears, and dizziness—he almost never tapped into it.

For Molly he would.

After five minutes of arguing, he gave in.

"You're gonna feel guilty," he said, "for making me suffer."

He was not totally serious. Molly counted on that being the fact. And so Clay positioned himself directly in front of the lampstand, bracing as if preparing to lift a piano on his shoulders. He closed his eyes. He slowed his breathing. He stiffened his jaw. He concentrated.

And some powerful mental shutter opened and closed.

His head jerked. His world was suddenly a gigantic tilt-a-whirl, and he was the only one riding on it. He reached out to Molly's bedrail to steady himself.

"So who'd ya see?"

Molly's voice came at him as if from a great distance. His stomach roiled, and the roar in his ears was a perfect imitation of a low-flying jet. His forehead felt as if someone had driven a stake into it.

When he was finally able to speak, he spoke very softly.

"A boy in a baseball cap."

"Hot darn, I knew it!" Molly exclaimed. "It's that pissant, Bradley. He's always pulling shitty tricks."

She pitched forward excitedly, and then, as if the movement deflated her, she sank back into her pillow and sighed. Still woozy himself, Clay handed her a weak smile.

"You want me to lay some hurt on him? Teach him not to mess with your goodies?"

"No, I'll get that little snotter—my own way."

Coming gradually out of his pain, Clay shook his head and tried to focus on the clock radio.

"Hey, it's sneaking up on nine. 'Bout time for our program."

Molly perked up a notch.

"Yeah, I'm ready." She hesitated and then wiggled her fingers at him. "Thanks, big brother—you feeling okay?"

He chuckled.

"Hell, no. My head feels like it has ground-up glass in it."

"Oh, you're bein' a darn wimp," she countered kiddingly. "Least you aren't dying."

Her words halted him for a second or two.

Then he smiled and switched on the radio.

"No, you're right. At least I'm not dying. But listen, don't ask me to do my weird thing again unless it's a lot more important than finding out who took your Milk Duds—you got me?"

"No problem," she said.

And her eyes flickered something like love.

Two

"Five minutes, Hillary."

"Thanks, Dave. I'm about ready to roll."

Hillary Garrett adjusted her headphones and smiled through the glass to the left of her booth at Dave Tanner, program engineer for station WPFX. Though Tanner was five or six years older than Hillary, she could tell that he was attracted to her. The fact that she was only sixteen had kept him at bay, she reasoned. Any day, she expected him to ask her out. In the reflection of the glass, she checked her short blond hair and her makeup before reminding herself that this was radio. *I could have tons of freckles and a mountain range of zits and no one would know.*

"Can you take a quick phone call?"

It was Tanner again, his smile showing beautifully white teeth.

"Yeah, but buzz through when I'm down to sixty seconds, okay?"

"Be glad to. Hope the show goes well this morning."

"Me, too," she replied, as much to herself as to Tanner.

She pressed the flashing red button on her phone and said, "This is Hillary Garrett. Hello."

"Good morning, Hillary. This is John Jaggery."

Hillary felt immediately and pleasantly warmed. The

voice on the other end of the line was as soothing as the sensation of sinking into a bubble bath, one of Hillary's favorite ways to relax.

"Oh, hi. It's great to hear from you. How are you liking retirement?"

"So far, so good. But you know me, I've got to be moving and shaking. Can't stand to twiddle my thumbs. I'm enjoying the lake, though I miss Velma like the dickens—doesn't seem that it's been two years since she passed away. She was more than a wife. She was a friend." The rhythm of his speech skipped a beat and then he continued. "And I dearly wish that I could learn to make a decent cup of coffee and wean myself from using the microwave so much. What about my number one Foxpath High student—what's it like to be a celebrity?"

Hillary laughed nervously and hoped it didn't sound too much like a girlish giggle.

"Celebrity? You've got to be kidding."

"No, my friend, I'm not. Earlier I talked with George Smith, your station manager, and he says the listener response to 'Just Pretend' has been terrific—all because of Hillary Garrett. And I want you to know, I've tuned in to all three of your shows and I'm among your most rabid fans."

"Thanks, Mr. Jaggery. That means a lot, especially because you went out of your way to help me get this job. I'm sure you were the best guidance counselor Foxpath High ever had. The school will miss you. All the kids will miss you. Me, first and most."

"You're very kind. And very deserving of your success. But as for my role at Foxpath High, well, thirty-five years was long enough—the school needs new blood." He paused, and Hillary thought she detected some regret in his tone. Then he added, "So, hey, the other reason I called is to let you know I'm sorry but that Bill, my Billy, won't be coming in for the taping with you. He's been under the weather, and he sends his regrets and says that he'll try to do it another time. Does that throw your schedule out of whack too much?"

"No, no," she said, her mind scanning a checklist of names. Bill Jaggery, an ex-Marine and a veteran of the Desert Storm campaign, had been slated for one of her regular program segments entitled, "What Grown-ups Do." "I have a woman plumber I can interview instead."

"Oh, good, good. Well, I know you must be about ready to go on the air, so I'll let you go. Hillary, you know, you're providing a real public service. Your show is wonderful for kids and for those of us adults who still feel like kids. Keep up the good work."

"Thanks. I do love kids, and if I can do something to help them, I will."

"I believe that," said Jaggery. "Say hello to your mom and dad for me. Good-bye now."

Hillary said good-bye, but when the warmth generated by Jaggery's voice had faded, she stared blankly at her hands.

Say hello to your mom and dad.

A frown pinched her forehead and the corners of her eyes, making her look ten years older. What her dear friend, Mr. Jaggery, did not realize was that, ironically, saying hello to her mom and dad was rather difficult these days.

Impossible at the moment.

Though it was nearly 9:00 on a Saturday morning,

Frances Garrett, her mother, would be asleep, or, more accurately, sleeping off her latest drunk. When Hillary had returned from a date last night, she had discovered her mother on the deck of their lake house crumpled up under a lounge chair, an empty, broken bottle of vodka near her head.

It was not the first time Hillary had dragged her mother to bed, or rather, to the living room couch, and, quite likely, unless her mother got some professional help right away, it wouldn't be the final time. After the exhausting struggle to get the oblivious woman inside, Hillary had fought back a welling of tears and called her father.

Tucker Garrett was a successful man.

As a business consultant, he made impressive sums of money each year, which had allowed him to build a veritable mansion on Foxpath Lake and to give his wife and daughter any luxury their hearts desired.

Except his time.

And himself.

Hillary caught up with him in Chicago.

"Daddy, she's done it again. When are you coming home? She needs help. Can't you convince her to check into a clinic?"

But that's not what she had wanted to say.

Can't you come home and be the husband she needs?

"Sugar babe, if I thought it would do any good, I'd catch a flight out tonight, but I can't *force* your mother to do the right thing. She has to want to, and I don't see signs she does. Now here's the thing: I have two, maybe three days of important work, and then I'll be home for a spell and we'll deal with this. You all right otherwise? Need anything?"

She had bitten her tongue.

Yes, she needed quite a lot.

Needed someone to repair a broken family.

"No. No, I'm fine. I'm just worried about Mom. I'm just afraid that one of these days she's going to drink too much and . . . I'm just real worried about her."

"I'm sure you are, babe, and so am I. I'll be home next week. That's a promise."

"Sixty seconds."

Dave Tanner's smile flickered and she nodded, slipping back to reality.

"I'm ready," she said, her tone distant, emotionless.

"Hey, is anything wrong?"

She manufactured a smile.

And began to think about her listeners. It seemed odd to her that she knew so few of them. Didn't know, for example, that a few miles away, Clay Brannon and his sister Molly were waiting for her show to begin.

She gave Tanner a thumbs-up.

He raised a hand, and the final countdown was underway.

"Good morning, boys and girls and everyone who still has a little bit of boy and girl within. This is Hillary Garrett coming to you on WPFX, 'Fox Radio,' and our program is called, 'Just Pretend.' It's a beautiful Saturday and we're going to have fun, just you wait and see."

And that's how things got underway.

Sixteen years old and her own half hour radio show.

Sometimes Hillary had to pinch herself because it seemed so improbable that "Just Pretend" was actually on the air, and yet she had worked hard to see the project materialize from a dream through a series of stages until the fateful day on which George Smith had reached across his desk to shake her hand and said, "You've done it, Hillary. Congratulations. 'Just Pretend' has sponsors and its own Saturday morning time slot."

Her critics claimed that kids wouldn't listen to radio, that her program couldn't possibly compete with television and video games, but Hillary was out to prove them wrong, for she believed her format could touch the imagination of kids in a way that nothing else could.

"On our 'Safety First' segment this morning we're going to talk about sunburn and wasp and bee stings and how you can avoid them and what you can do to make the 'ouch' go away if you don't avoid them."

Having consulted local health officials, including a physician or two, Hillary informed her listeners in language they could understand, gently admonishing them as well about the potential dangers of staying out in the sun too long and of being stung by a wasp or bee.

After a long commercial break, she offered a review of the movie *Jurassic Park,* and, in doing so, tackled the sensitive issue of whether the film might be too frightening for younger children. Having viewed it twice, Hillary suggested that it was probably too intense for kids under eight.

"If you have your heart set on seeing this movie, talk it over with your parents and listen to what they have to say. You can trust their judgment."

When they're sober.

Hillary quickly pushed thoughts of her mother aside

and opened the phone line for callers, inviting kids who had seen *Jurassic Park* to share their views of it.

The segment went well.

As always, Hillary marveled at how rapidly time passed during the airing of the program. It seemed to her that she had just said good morning when she glanced over at Tanner who was signaling for the final segment to begin.

Her favorite segment.

The heart of "Just Pretend."

It was a regular feature in which she emphasized to her young listeners that they possessed a tremendous power, a power that, much like physical muscle, could actually be strengthened through exercise.

The power of the imagination.

And the attendant delight of "pretending."

She did, of course, hasten to add that no one should spend so much time pretending that he or she would miss out on the real joys of everyday reality.

But a little of it was good. And a lot of fun.

In this segment, she also opened the phone line, this time inviting callers to share what they had been pretending. On this particular morning, the calls reflected the kind of pleasant vividness Hillary hoped for.

"This is 'Just Pretend.' You're on the air, caller. What is your name and what have you been pretending?"

"Hi . . . well, my name's Brian, and I been pretending I'm a rock."

"A rock?" Hillary smiled, one hand on her headphone so that she could hear more clearly. "What kind of rock?"

"A flat rock. See, I been pretending I'm a flat rock on the shore by a lake. A big lake."

"Oh, that sounds interesting. And so you just lie around

on the shore by that big lake—doesn't that get kind of boring?"

"No, 'cause you know what happens?"

"I guess I don't, but I want you to tell me and all our listeners."

"Well, see, what I do is I wait around for somebody to come walking along looking for rocks."

"Somebody who's collecting rocks?"

"Not 'collecting.' Not really. See, I'm waiting for somebody who's looking for a flat rock, you know, for a good skippin' rock."

"Oh, of course. Flat rocks skip on the water much better than round ones, don't they?"

"Yeah. Yeah, and see it's real fun when they pick me up and throw me and I just skip and skip and skip on the water. I bet I'd skip five or six or eight times maybe. And that's what I pretend."

"And it doesn't hurt you when you get thrown across the water?"

"No. No, because, see, you can't hurt rocks, and see it's okay when they sink in the lake because rocks can't drown, you know."

"Hmm, I guess you're right about that. Well, Brian, that's a very interesting thing to pretend you are. Thank you for calling, and if you'll give me your phone number someone here at the station will be calling you back to get your address because you know what?"

"No, what?"

"For being our first caller on our 'Just Pretend' segment this morning, we're going to send you a coupon for a free pizza at Pizza World. How does that sound?"

"Pretty nice. It sounds pretty nice."

There were three other callers, the first two every ounce as charming and innocently creative as the boy who pretended to be a rock. A little girl named Jana described the experience of pretending to be a goldfish, and a boy named Tyson had pretended to be a young sweet gum tree and shared the sensations of various weather changes from clear and sunny to windy and rainy.

The calls tugged at Hillary's heart.

But nothing could have prepared her for the final caller.

With time running out, Tanner caught her attention.

"You maybe have a minute and a half to take one more."

Hillary hesitated.

"What the heck," she said while a commercial was playing. "Yeah, put it through."

"You're on."

"Hello," she said when the "On Air" sign flashed. "This is 'Just Pretend.' What is your name and what have you been pretending?"

Loud breathing. But no response.

"Caller? You're on the air. Can you give us your name?"

A whisper. The words not quite audible.

"I can't hear you and we haven't much time," she prodded.

Suddenly a soft voice broke through. A little girl's voice.

"Help me."

Hillary bolted upright. She glanced through the glass at Tanner. He was frowning. Hillary felt an immediate sensation of numbness.

"Who is this, please? Honey, is there something wrong? Did you say you need help?"

She held her breath as she waited for a response.

"I pretended . . ."

Hillary listened with an intensity which made her body ache. There was unmistakable fear in the voice at the other end of the line.

"Yes, go on. You pretended what? Honey, go on."

A score of agonizing seconds passed. And then.

"I pretended a bad man . . . and he . . ."

Hillary swallowed hard. Something in that voice terrified her.

"Honey, maybe you shouldn't pretend things that will scare you."

She chided herself for saying that. It sounded trite. She suddenly noticed that other station personnel had gathered near her booth to listen to the bizarre call.

"Help me . . . I pretended a bad man . . ."

Feeling a razor edge of desperation cutting into her, Hillary said, "Please tell me who you are and where you're calling from and what kind of help you need. Please. Please, yes, I want to help you."

"I'm in a phone booth . . . at the lake."

"Good, honey. Okay, now, tell me what's wrong. You sound very frightened. Please. You can tell me."

Another pause. This one seemed to last an eternity.

Then some final words from the caller.

Words which ushered Hillary Garrett into a nightmare unlike any other she had ever experienced.

"I pretended a bad man . . . and he's going to kill me."

Three

The stone read, "Gone to Be an Angel."

Clay Brannon stared down at it, caressed by the velvet melancholy he always felt in the small, anonymous graveyard not far from Foxpath Lake or from the mobile home where he and his mother lived.

Long ago, he and Molly had dubbed this weed-choked, scrubby pine area "The Children's Graveyard" for obvious reasons: of the two dozen or so gravesites, the markers—many of them broken or with worn lettering—indicated that most of the individuals buried here were children. The new asphalt road which snaked around Foxpath Lake took travelers by the graveyard, but Clay knew that very, very few knew the somber plots existed. A passerby would have to slow and look in earnest to spot a headstone, though some might take note of the tiny, gray-weathered gravehouse with its peaked roof and broken-toothed lathing and diminutive, obelisk monument.

For Clay and Molly the graveyard was a special place.

In days past, they had spent hours haunting it, fascinated by the untold tales, the unrecorded dramas each grave held. Molly liked to clean the headstones and clip the grass and weeds away from them, and, of course, she loved to speculate on the cause of death for each resident. Sometimes she would turn to Clay and point down at a headstone and say, "Here lies Perry O. Davis: born July 4, 1907, died November 23, 1910. Tell me his story."

And Clay would.

It would be a purple narrative filled with mystery and passion and romance and tragedy. Most of the time Clay's fictional narratives sketched out loving parents heartbroken over the death of their "only beloved," their "Angel on Earth," their child who succumbed to yellow fever or smallpox, or perhaps to snakebite or even to some mysterious act of God bordering on the supernatural. For many of the deaths Clay inserted the possibility that the child's ghost lingered near its grave as if merely waiting for its parents to arrive.

But on that warm Saturday afternoon in June, Clay had come to the graveyard to think. He had left the hospital and pedaled his tenspeed along the four-mile route to the lake, hoping that the ride would put a certain ghostly voice behind him. In the shade of some sweet gums, he sat down on a headstone which read, "Opal Louise Gunnert/ We Loved Her, But God Loved Her More" and thought about the radio program "Just Pretend"—and mostly about that final caller.

I pretended a bad man, and he's going to kill me.

Wasn't that what the caller had said?

He and Molly had looked at each other in stunned silence. When the program signed off the air, he had said, "Do you think that kid's pulling a prank?"

To which Molly had responded, "No, I don't think so. It's really weird. But I don't think it's a prank. No kid's that good an actor, 'cept me, of course."

They had both chuckled. But the caller had touched a

nerve in them, and Clay found himself agreeing with Molly. The caller had sounded extremely convincing.

And very frightened.

It had been obvious that Hillary Garrett was frightened, too, but Clay felt she had handled the situation with admirable calm. Although he and Hillary both had just finished their junior year at Foxpath High School, he didn't know her. He recalled that they had had a course (was it English?) or two together, and yet he hadn't paid much attention to her because she moved in a glitzy circle—and her parents had built one of the finest homes on the lake.

No, Hillary Garrett was definitely not his type.

Pushing her from his thoughts, Clay glanced down at a fire ant mound constructed atop one of the graves.

Not the Conqueror Worm, but the Conqueror Ant, he mused.

And he wondered whether the young caller was really being threatened by someone. From that thought it was an easy transition to thoughts of Molly—dear Molly, stalked by the real and deadly threat of cancer.

Will she ever be able to come to our graveyard again?

He wouldn't allow himself to doubt it.

"Damn it, I can't give up hope," he whispered aloud. "Oh, Molly, you just can't die."

But he knew that she might.

Suddenly, off to his left from the depth of the woods, he heard something. Someone? Yes, someone calling out a name. He stood up and held his breath and listened. And the calling edged closer until the underbrush beyond the graveyard parted and a man emerged.

And walked straight toward Clay.

"Priddy Ann? Hey, you. Hey, you, mister. Have you

seen Priddy Ann? She's my sister. I heard her crying for help. Have you seen her? She's about this tall."

The man leveled his hand about four feet above the ground.

Clay shook his head and released his breath, relieved that he knew the man. It was Jeremiad "Jeremy" Ketch, and Clay had known him—or at least seen him around the lake—for years. Ketch, often referred to as the "Foxpath Fiend," stared at Clay with a near desperation stare. The man was short with dark brown curly hair, a heavy beard, a slight limp, and wore a ragged, dirty blue jumpsuit, the same clothes he wore every day. When younger, Clay had always been scared of Ketch, for in truth the man—no one seemed to know his age—had been in and out of mental institutions and could not hold a job. He lived in a shotgun shack with his mother and roamed the woods and sometimes rowed a boat on the lake—by himself.

"If you see her," said Ketch. "If you see my sister, Priddy Ann, you tell her I be lookin' for her. I'm her brother, Jeremy, and I be lookin' for her. I got her 'bun-bun'. You see it?"

Ketch held out a stuffed toy bunny with one ear missing; the sight of it jogged Clay into recalling that the "Foxpath Fiend" was fond of stuffed animals.

But was he truly dangerous?

Some thought he was. Some thought he wouldn't hurt a fly.

Clay nodded again.

"I haven't seen your sister, but if I do I'll tell her I saw you. I'll tell her to go on home."

Ketch's eyes brightened.

"Yeah, that'll do. Tell her, 'You go on home, Priddy Ann.' Yeah, that'll do."

The man smiled a maniacal smile, revealing crooked teeth; his face seemed to take on an eerie glow, and then before Clay could add anything, the man tromped off noisily into the woods. As far as Clay knew, the man did not have a little sister, or any other family besides his mother.

Clay stood and watched the spot where Ketch had disappeared, and then he noticed that he was trembling. He felt like a small boy again, for the Foxpath Fiend had not lost his capacity for terrifying him.

What is it about that guy?

Those eyes? He scares the hell out of me.

But there was no time to ponder the matter. Clay needed to run by home, then by the hospital, and then on to Kroger's for the six to midnight shift in the produce department.

When he walked into his family's mobile home a few minutes later, he was greeted by air that was as warm as the midday heat.

"Is the air conditioner on the fritz again?"

His mother, Dora Brannon, looked up from her sewing; her mouth was set grimly.

"It died yesterday. Can we have someone to fix it?"

Clay worked at the dials of the dusty window unit and then gave the side of it a hard slap. He shook his head.

"No point. I think it's beyond repair, and we sure can't afford a new one. Why don't you have the fan set up on you?"

As he waited for his mother's reply, he mentally wrote down the air conditioner on the long list of things they would have to do without. Although he was working full-time and his mother part-time, they barely met monthly expenses. Molly's health problems had broken them financially, and Clay knew only too well that most of her medical bills would never be paid.

"The heat's not so bad once you get yourself used to it. Folks nowadays are spoiled. Too many comforts. When your father and I was first married, we never had no air conditioning or things like that. And we got along just fine, and so we can get along just fine now."

Clay went to the refrigerator and drank directly from a jar of ice water. He wondered what kind of afternoon Molly was having. She needed rest. He hoped the "heme" team wouldn't make an unexpected visit to her while she was trying to sleep.

Back in the living room, he started to ask his mother a question about the Foxpath Fiend, about whether she had ever heard anything of the Ketch family having a little girl. But when he noticed what his mother was sewing, all he could do was grit his teeth and clench his fists.

He calmed himself enough to speak, his words coming out in a flat whisper.

"What are you doing?"

Puzzled, his mother glanced up, pushing her glasses higher on her nose. She shrugged.

"Sewing on a button. They get pulled off or just come off on their own, you know."

Clay reached for the plaid workshirt in her lap. It was his father's shirt and the sight of it disgusted him.

"Why?" he said, tugging angrily at the shirt. "Why are you wasting time on this?"

Wresting the shirt violently from his grasp, his mother snapped, "Your daddy's gone need this when he gets back.

He don't hardly have no shirts that ain't tore up. Several needs mendin' and that's what I been doin' and it's not wastin' time, so don't tell me it is."

Clay hunkered down in front of his mother. His voice softened.

"Mom, he's not . . . he's not going to come back."

Refusing to meet his eyes, she continued sewing, but he could see that her entire body was responding to what he had to say. Her shoulders were quaking, and her mouth twitched defiantly. She was listening but pretending not to.

Touching her knee, Clay said, "It's just like in that play we read at school. Just like in *The Glass Menagerie* where the father leaves. He fell in love with long distances and left the mother and the son and the daughter. That's what happened."

"No," said his mother in a tense, tear-choked voice, "it's not like no play. Your father has gone to Louisiana to find work. You know there's nothin' around here. He tried pulpwooding and couldn't make a go of it, and so if he can get on with one of them oil rigs down there things'd be fine. He's been sendin' us money right along."

Clay offered a dispirited smile.

"Mom, he's been gone for over a year, and in all that time he's sent money twice—forty dollars both times. What does that cover—groceries for a week? Mom, some of those medications Molly takes cost more than forty dollars a bottle."

Tears were beginning to trickle from the corners of her eyes, and yet she continued sewing.

"Why you got to be so down on your father? He's tryin' his best. He calls regular like."

"It's funny he never calls when I'm here. And I can't forgive him for not coming back to see Molly. That's the least he could do. *One* of her parents should be visiting her."

He instantly regretted that remark.

Dora Brannon was a weak woman who loved her derelict husband desperately. She loved her children, too, and yet there was something about Molly's condition which appeared to have severed the maternal cord connecting her to her daughter.

"You know I'd like to," she said. "You know I will. You tell our Molly I'll be seein' her soon. Will you do that?"

She reached up from her sewing and patted his cheek.

Clay nodded and gestured for her to get back to what she was doing. He knew he couldn't repair a broken family.

"I have to go," he said. "I'm going to stop by to see Molly before I go to work. I'll be late."

"Don't you want a little somethin' to eat? I can fix you a bite."

He shook his head.

"I'll pick up something at work."

He kept the Snickers bar he had bought from one of the hospital's vending machines behind his back as he entered Molly's room. Hands washed and mask in place, he waded into the delicately hammering sound of Jimi Hendrix's "Purple Haze," and Molly met him with the best smile she could muster. She was wearing a psychedelic headband sporting the 60s slogan "Make Love Not

War," but no wig. Her bald head was blue-veined, and to Clay she looked like a gigantic yet extremely fragile egg.

"Hey, Queen Mab," he said, pulling down his mask after checking over his shoulder for any sign of nurses in the area.

"Hi ya, Cabby." She motioned for him to turn down Hendrix. "I just woke up from a nap. Seems like I sleep all the time these days. I was thinking about how to get back at that snothead Bradley for walking off with my chocolate."

"You thought of anything good and nasty?"

"Not yet. Hey, you think I look too gross without a wig on? The nurses freak over the headband. What do you think?"

"Hmm," said Clay, gazing at her as if he were studying an art object. "I think you look sexy."

Molly beamed.

"Too sexy for all the boys on this ward—for the girls, too. You ever notice how some girls are really shitty?"

"Some, yeah."

"But not Hillary Garrett, right?"

Clay sensed that his sister was orchestrating something.

"You mean the radio host? Let's just say she's not my type."

"Why not?"

"Several reasons: her folks are filthy rich, she's 'Miss Everything' at school, travels in all the right circles, and is too much of a goody-goody—into a lot of causes, but I don't think she's really serious about them. We have nothing in common."

"She likes kids."

"Why you asking me about her?"

Molly looked away.

"Her show this morning—that little girl who called, the one who pretended a bad man. I keep thinking about her."

"Me, too. Strange business, huh?"

"Yeah, super strange."

"Speaking of super strange, guess who I ran into at the Children's Graveyard?"

"One of those ghosts you made up for me?"

"Somebody even scarier."

Molly wrinkled her nose.

"The Foxpath Fiend?"

"In the flesh. He was carrying around this stuffed toy rabbit, and he was looking for his little sister. His face was all crazy. You should've seen him."

"Yeah, he's as scary as Freddy Krueger or Hannibal the Cannibal. I sure wouldn't want . . ."

Molly was frowning. And the distant light in her eyes—Clay had often seen it when his sister was deep into a problem or projecting dark possibilities.

"What is it? You sure wouldn't want what?"

Five seconds passed.

And then Molly turned, lines of seriousness—and perhaps fear—etched at the corners of her mouth.

"Cab, do you think the Foxpath Fiend would ever kill somebody?"

Another five seconds passed before Clay could respond.

Four

"Yes," said Hillary, "if there's any lemonade, but Charmian, don't go to any special effort for me. I just want to sit here and unwind."

Charmian Hornsby, who had been employed as the Garrett's maid all six years they had lived at the lake, smiled gently. She had asked Hillary whether she wanted something cold to drink on such a warm evening.

"No trouble, honey. I made up a pitcher this afternoon so's there'd be some when you got home. Your momma, she don't drink lemonade. There's a full pitcher. Would you like a sandwich, too?"

"No, thanks. Do you know whether Mother has eaten anything?"

"I 'spect not, miss. She's mostly just been sleeping. I did my dusting upstairs and downstairs quiet like a mouse so's I wouldn't wake her none."

Hillary frowned.

"She really needs to eat something or she'll be sick. I should have checked on her when I came home, but I've had a lot on my mind."

Reclining on a lounge chair on the Garrett's impressive deck, Hillary gazed at the surface of Foxpath Lake which was burnished by the approach of sunset. It was such a peaceful and serene setting that it made her ache with a desire to transform her inner chaos to a similar state of serenity. By degrees she became aware that Charmian, hands on hips, was watching her.

"Honey, I knowed that something was troubling you. You need to tell Charmian about it?"

Hillary smiled.

She reached out and squeezed the woman's wrist.

"Thanks for being concerned, but, no, this is a matter I have to wrestle with on my own. And, oh, before I forget, has Dad called today?"

"No'm." The woman paused, and the twilight painted a gold sheen on her black face and hair and arms. "It's a pure shame Mr. Garrett work so hard he don't never have time to enjoy this place. He should be right here with you looking at that pretty sunset."

"I know," said Hillary.

Charmian sighed heavily and walked away.

Hillary swung around to immerse herself in the view, a view that everyone on Foxpath Lake envied. To her left about half a mile, the shoreline thrust out to a point; there were no houses or cabins; deep woods concealed a series of caves, one of which had actually been a moderately profitable gold mine years ago. To her right, the shoreline showed signs of new development, and where another point extended like an index finger, Hillary could see the home of John Jaggery.

She wondered suddenly what Jaggery thought of this morning's "Just Pretend." She wondered, in fact, what all of her listeners thought.

I pretended a bad man, and he's going to kill me.

She could not stop thinking about those words, that voice.

But she had spent late morning and nearly the entire afternoon trying to find the caller. The Foxpath police, while receptive to her concerns, weren't able to offer much help. She was told that the department lacked the technical capacity to trace a call from a phone booth unless there had been special preparation beforehand.

They also reminded her that such a call could well have been a hoax. Some little girl with an overactive imagination.

But it wasn't. I just know it wasn't.

She had no proof. Only her intuition.

And her intuition told her something horrible might occur.

Or already had.

Although it was a needle in a haystack situation, she had driven around the lake most of the afternoon, locating six public phone booths and questioning nearly a dozen people to determine whether anyone had seen a small girl in or near a phone booth that morning.

She turned up nothing.

"This is a nightmare," she whispered to herself.

Charmian brought her a large glass of lemonade and asked whether she needed anything else.

"Thanks, no."

"I'll be going for home, then," said Charmian. "But donchoo be worrying yourself over something all night, y'hear? Worry—it's like that ole lake out there. You could dip out buckets of it everyday and by the time you be old as me, that ole lake still be full of water."

Hillary nodded.

"I think I see what you're saying. Thanks."

She stood up and gave Charmian a hug and they said good night.

Twilight settled.

Leaning against the railing of the deck, Hillary drank in the rising splendor of a full moon. It silvered the landscape, deepening the impression of tranquility.

I pretended a bad man, and he's going to kill me.

Hillary closed her eyes and clenched her fists.

I feel so damn helpless.

So completely had she surrendered to her anguish that she did not hear footsteps behind her until the visitor was within fifty feet. Then she turned quickly, startled to see a man she could not recognize immediately.

"Hillary?"

An outline materialized. The voice familiar. Then the face.

Relieved, she pressed the palm of one hand to her throat.

"Oh, Mr. Jaggery . . . oh, I didn't hear you."

"My dear, I must have frightened you. I'm very sorry. Are you okay?"

His expression was a mask of concern, but when he saw that she had recovered, he began to smile. Hillary gestured for him to sit. Although his face was flecked with liver spots and his glasses were thick and the rims large and black, giving him the look of an owl, to Hillary it was a kindly face, a face you could trust. He was wearing a white golf cap and a dark jumpsuit and sneakers.

"No, I'm fine. Are you out on your evening stroll?"

"Yes, it's such a lovely night I couldn't resist. That moon. Have you ever seen a brighter moon? Can you believe that anyone has ever associated the moon with evil?

That it turns people into werewolves and such? How could that kind of notion come out of something so beautiful?"

"A good question. Say, can I get you some lemonade? Charmian's made a whole pitcher, and you've tasted her lemonade before—good stuff."

"I have, and it's terrific. But thanks, no. I was merely walking this way and saw the deck lights on and I was feeling lonely. Thought I'd seek out company. Evenings like this, I can't help missing my Velma. A wonderful companion, she was."

"I'm glad you stopped by. Is your son better? You said he hadn't been feeling well."

"He's better, yes. And your folks, how are they? Your dad has promised a golf game if he ever lights here long enough to get out on the links."

"You know Dad—busy, busy. He must love what he's doing because he certainly puts a lot of time, a lot of himself, into it."

"Look what he's earned for his labors."

Jaggery gestured widely, sweeping his hands out as if to mark the circumference of the house and grounds.

"But it's like Charmian was saying to me earlier—he's never here to enjoy it."

Jaggery nodded solemnly.

"What's your mom up to these days?"

Hillary smirked.

"Keeping the liquor stores in business."

An awkward silence stole upon the scene. Night insects droned. Miffed at herself for the remark, Hillary tried to find words to cover the embarrassment—hers and Jaggery's—and yet she assumed that he—that virtually everyone on Foxpath Lake—was aware that Frances Garrett had a serious drinking problem.

"Sorry," Hillary followed. "It's just that Mom's situation angers me as well as frightens me. I don't know how to help her."

His hands folded together as if he were about to pray, Jaggery hesitated a moment longer and then said, "That's just it—you can't help her. It's like they say: a person has to want to help themselves. It's doubly hard, though, if that person is someone you love."

Suddenly Hillary felt a welling of tears in her throat. But she fought them off. It was comforting to have Jaggery there, to be close to a man of sensitivity and understanding. She believed she could trust him as she moved the conversation into another thorny area.

"Did you listen to my program this morning?" she asked.

"Yes, indeed, and . . . well, that's the other reason I dropped by this evening. I got to thinking you were probably deeply troubled by that final caller."

"It was horrible."

She went on to recount her attempts to trace the call and to track down the caller, punctuating her summary with a heartfelt observation.

"I feel responsible," she said. "It was my idea to have the segment in the first place. And now . . . what if in some way I've *caused* this to happen. What if that little girl really does have someone in her life who's trying to harm her?"

Jaggery smiled benignly.

"But you can't hold yourself responsible for that. At the very worst, the child's imagination may have taken a dark turn and spawned some shadowy figure lurking in her closet or under her bed—but not a *real* someone. She may have given herself a bad dream or two. What child hasn't? Why, my guess is that by this evening she's forgotten the whole business. Or has talked with her parents, who, by the way, probably weren't even aware she called your program."

"You make it all sound so innocent. Your explanation is convincing, and yet . . . I don't know. I have a bad feeling. Could it be a child's way of talking about being abused? Should I go see a child psychologist about this?"

"If it would ease your mind, yes, perhaps so. But I question whether it's really necessary. You do so much good for children. Don't let this one incident sway you from your mission."

She wanted to believe he was right.

Thoughts in a dark swirl, she grinned when he patted her hand reassuringly. She felt somewhat better.

And yet when she went to bed that night, demons of doubt returned to meet her at the edge of sleep.

"What's this all about?"

Hillary had slipped into Dave Tanner's booth. It was the next day—a Sunday afternoon—a very unusual time for the station manager to call her in for a meeting.

Removing his headphones, Tanner smiled at first when he saw her, but when he spoke he seemed anxious and unsure—the verbal equivalent of walking on eggs.

"Beats me, except . . . we've been getting some calls about your show yesterday. Quite a few calls . . . and they have George concerned. I mean, when you get calls from mothers, you know, that's a problem."

"Well, what are they saying?"

"Hey, I'm just repeating what I heard. I don't have specifics. George is concerned, and that's why he asked me to call you in."

"Has there been some word on that little girl who called?"

Tanner shrugged.

"Not that I'm aware of. Wow, I mean, that call was freaky deaky, wasn't it?"

Hillary folded her arms against her chest. George Smith wanted to meet with her at 2:00 and it was three minutes till. Back at the lake, she had fixed her mother some lunch and had been pleased to see her up and looking more on top of things, wearing makeup and a tattered smile. Her mother, despite some damaging effects of alcohol, was still capable of presenting herself as a beautiful woman when she wanted to.

Nodding at Tanner, Hillary glanced impatiently at her watch and then at the station manager's closed door.

"Might as well go face the music. Wish me luck."

Tanner tried to smile. She reasoned he knew just how harsh that music would sound.

George Smith also tried to smile.

Behind his imposing desk, he shuffled through some papers even as he invited her in. A sixtyish man with thinning gray hair scalped to resemble a crewcut, Smith had a florid face and bags under his eyes. He and his office smelled like smoke. Hillary silently predicted that the combination of smoking and being overweight would be the downfall of the man before too much longer.

"You won't believe this," he began, "but the top of this desk was clean on Friday afternoon." He shuffled a few more papers and reached for a manila folder. "I apologize for needin' to have you come in on a Sunday and all, but . . . couldn't be helped. We got to talk."

Hillary squirmed in a leather chair which threatened to swallow her. Knowing how Smith liked to circle an issue before attacking it, she decided to help him speed up the process.

"This is about 'Just Pretend,' isn't it?"

He looked up from his paper shuffling and, for the blink of an eye, seemed embarrassed.

"Yes, ma'am, it is."

He rubbed his stubby fingers together and contorted his mouth almost comically. But before he could add anything, Hillary said, "I don't think it was a hoax, Mr. Smith. I really don't have a clue as to what's going on with that little girl, but her call convinced me it's something serious."

"I expect you could be right," he said. "Who can say? Fact of the matter is, we just maybe'll never know. Now, what I've got to say to you concerns your show and not so much that caller, though they're related."

"Dave said the station's been getting calls."

"Yes, ma'am, and some folks are upset and that's the main reason you and I need to talk."

"Are the police continuing to look into this?"

Smith waved off her question.

"No, now, you see, our business is one thing and police business is a whole 'nother thing. These folks calling in— and they're mostly parents, mostly mothers—why, they're very upset about what happened on the air yesterday."

"Well, of course," said Hillary. "They should be. That little girl—"

"Now wait a second. They're more concerned about their own kids. You see what I mean?"

"No. No, I don't."

Smith puffed out his cheeks and tapped his fingers on the desktop.

"You scared their kids. That's what I mean."

"*I* scared . . ."

"What these folks are saying is, they don't want that segment to be included in your program no more. Now that's the fact of the matter, and that's what you and me got to talk about."

Hillary felt her entire body bristle.

Her throat was suddenly scratchy and dry.

"But that segment is the heart of my show."

"I'm aware of that, I am. But, you see, when enough folks get upset about something on the air and they start making demands and start mentioning our sponsors, well . . . you see where we are."

Hillary sat and shook her head; she was angry and hurt, and she was determined—if it took every ounce of her strength—not to cry and not to allow her voice to crack.

"So what do you want me to do?"

Smith had the anguished look of a man who did not have a settled position on the matter but needed to state one in the next few seconds.

"Well, first off, Hillary, I want you to work with me on this. How'd it be if we drop the 'pretend' segment? What I mean is, no sense throwing the baby out with the bath water—you've got a real fine show. Real fine. A number of other good segments. Just sorta phase out the segment folks are upset about."

The word came out of Hillary's mouth automatically. She said it intensely, yet so low it was barely audible.

"No."

His tongue pressed hard against his upper row of teeth, Smith appeared surprised.

"Won't you just think about it, and let's maybe talk again middle of the week?"

"No. No . . . it won't matter. I won't change my mind. That segment makes the show what it is. I'm torn by this because I'm worried about that little girl. But there's no show without that segment—not the show I want on the air."

Smith leaned back, his face flushed. He was anticipating pain for both of them.

"All right, then. I got no choice. Your show's canceled for the time being. I just wish to thunder you'd consider a compromise of some kind."

Hillary felt empty.

"No. No compromise," she said. She squared up her shoulders and stiffened her chin. "Pull the show if that's what you have to do."

Five

Molly was wearing a raccoon skin cap.

Grinning behind his hospital mask, Clay approached her sleeping form and saw a dribble of saliva escaping from one corner of her mouth. The tail of her furry cap was curled along her throat like a much-loved pet.

A jolt of love hit Clay in the chest.

Molly looked so precious. So peaceful. How could it be that the "sharks" of leukemia, as she called them, were eating her alive, turning her blood rotten and consuming all the good, life-giving cells?

It seemed beyond possibility.

Yet, everywhere he turned he crashed into evidence to support that possibility.

Yesterday, a Monday, he had been visiting her during the morning when she developed a severe nosebleed. Dr. Winston had been on call, and before he left Molly's room after attending to her, he had allowed an expression of grim acceptance to steal across his face.

Clay had witnessed that expression.

He translated it into one simple sentence: *The end is near.*

Today, Molly appeared paler than he had ever seen her.

A ghost of a ghost of a ghost, Clay thought to himself as he leaned over her and reached out for the paperback on her lampstand. It was *The Vampire Lestat,* one of the books in Anne Rice's vampire chronicles. Molly loved fictional vampires—the real ones, members of the "heme" team, were another matter entirely.

Clay strained not to make her stir.

"Can't a girl get her beauty rest?"

He jumped back at Molly's sudden comment; she was awake, smiling weakly, her eyes bloodshot, one faint blue vein stitched down her jaw.

"Damn, I'm sorry I woke you," he said.

Molly sighed.

"I'm weaker 'an a cat," she said.

"Just hold on. I think you're getting stronger."

"That what Dr. Winston said?"

She had him there. Clay played with his hands as if he were shuffling cards. He shuffled words, instead.

"You know doctors . . . they don't say much. Too afraid they'll be wrong. Or get sued."

"He thinks I'm dead meat."

"Who does?"

"Winston. Yeah, he does. I can see it in his eyes. I see little skulls where his pupils should be."

Clay grimaced.

"Would you stop that," he said. He wanted to change the subject. "Where'd you get the Daniel Boone cap?"

Molly rolled her eyes up as if only then aware of what she was wearing.

"Oh, that. From Bradley's pissant younger brother, Trevor."

"He just give it to you?"

Molly smiled wickedly.

"Not exactly. He came bopping in here last night when

no nurses were around and he dared me to put it on. So, you see, I did. And then he wanted it back and I said, 'Okay, but now anybody who wears this cap will get cancer just like me.' Guess what? He lost interest in his cap."

"Molly, geez, that was mean. Probably gave the kid nightmares.

"Yeah."

Molly laughed first. Then Clay joined her.

For a moment, just a moment, there was a sparkle of strong light in Molly's eyes. Like a firefly in a deep, dark night. Clay wished he could capture it, keep it, protect it, and make sure it was always there to signal that the life-force would never die in his sister.

Molly glanced down near his foot and said, "You brought your notebook. Read me what you been writing."

"Nothing worth hearing," he said. "Scribbles mostly. Personal stuff, you know."

Molly rubbed her hands together gleefully, nearly pulling one of her IVs loose.

"Sexual fantasies, I bet. Come on, let me hear 'em."

"It's not about me."

Squinting at him, Molly said, "Is it about *me?*"

"Yeah. Well, sorta."

"You gotta let me hear it, then. Come on. Please. It's the least you could do for a dying woman."

"Molly. Hey, damn it, I wish you wouldn't kid about that."

"About what?"

"You know."

"Read to me."

"All right, all right. But this piece is real rough. I've

just started it, and I'm not sure where it's going. It's . . . it's sort of a fairy tale and I call it, 'The Girl Who Sailed Away.' "

Molly softly repeated the words.

"That's a cool title," she said.

With the notebook open, Clay glanced up at her to measure whether it was a good idea to read what he had written. He wasn't sure. But he began. "This is a story about the girl who sailed away on a sea no one else had ever sailed. She sailed away because she had to. It was time for her to do so. And no one else had ever sailed upon that sea because there was no one else like this particular girl. That sea existed only for her. A sea of her very own. And she had built a special boat for her voyage, a boat like no one else's. And she—"

"Knock, knock, Molly-walla-doodle-all-day, it's 'Mr. Chocolate.' Tell your brother to put away his drugs and I won't squeal to the nurses."

Molly clenched her fists and yelled, "Bradley, you snot-licker, what do you want? And listen, my brother doesn't do drugs."

A chubby, sweaty-faced boy wearing an Atlanta Braves baseball cap and a Chicago Bulls T-shirt slouched into the room holding out a jar filled with Hershey's Kisses.

"Sorry I called you a druggie," he said to Clay as he shouldered up to the bed. "I brought you a peace offering, Molly, 'cause I know you're planning some bad shit on me for stealing your Duds—'cept I didn't *steal* 'em. It was more like *borrowing* 'em. I was gonna pay you back. Honest."

Clay could tell that the boy was probably on the pudgy side as a result of being on Prednisone, a steroid used in the treatment of leukemia—"makes you eat like a pig and act like a brat"—was Molly's characterization of the drug.

"Yeah, pay me back when I was sleeping with worms," said Molly. But she accepted the Hershey's Kisses and unwrapped one for herself and one for Clay. Bradley tore the wrapper off two, jammed them into his mouth and said, "You hear about the dead girl? They found her up at the old gold mine up at the lake. Man, it's like she'd been strangled all to death. It was really gruesome."

Clay felt an odd twinge high in his stomach. Molly wrinkled her nose and said, "Is this like when you dreamed there were dead people stacked up in front of your door and you couldn't get out? And one tried to kiss you. Remember that? You're just being morbid, Bradley. Plain ole morbid. There's no dead girl."

"Oh, yes there is. This wasn't no dream. Just go and ask Nurse Blackburn. Her husband's a deputy sheriff. Go ask her. A girl got strangled. Go ask her."

"Do they have any idea who did it?" asked Clay.

The boy shrugged.

"Probably one of them weirdo serial killers," he said. Then, leaving the jar of candy with Molly, he started to back out of the room. "But you don't got to worry," he said to her, " 'cause baldheaded girls don't turn him on."

Molly spat an obscenity at him and he was gone.

A few minutes later, while she and Clay were listening to an old rock 'n roll tape—Clay being out of the mood to read anything more to her—Molly said, "Cab, you thinkin' the same thing I'm thinkin'?"

He hesitated. There was no point in trying to bullshit his sister—she was too sharp for that.

"Yeah, I suppose I am. I mean, I'm thinking maybe

that girl was the one, you know . . . who called the radio show. But it could just be a coincidence. It *could* be."

"It's not," said Molly. "I got a bad feeling it's not a coincidence."

For another score of minutes they talked around the subject of the murdered girl, half hoping that Bradley was wrong or lying, sensing, however, that he had delivered the truth.

"You want to listen to a tape?" Clay asked, unable to clear his mind of the horrid image of a little girl's body lying crumpled up in one of the caves of the gold mine area.

Molly shook her head.

"I'm wondering about something," she said.

"What's that?"

He didn't like her tone. It had a touch of eeriness in it.

"Well, I was wondering . . . if they have trouble catching the killer, well, I've got a question for you."

"Ask away."

"The thing you can do, you know . . . how you see who's been somewhere when they're not there anymore. Like how you saw it was Bradley who had taken my candy. I was wondering if you would be able to . . ."

She didn't need to finish.

Clay felt a coating of frost inch down his throat. His heart beat numbly as if suddenly too cold to work properly. He fumbled for some words as the chill spread throughout his body.

"I maybe could, but it would be . . . just too mindboggling, Molly. Just too mindboggling to try to deal with."

* * *

Hillary was finding the airport entranceways difficult to negotiate. It was late Tuesday evening, and she had spent from mid-afternoon on shopping at one of the area malls to get her mind off George Smith's decision.

"Just Pretend" had been cut.

Unwilling to compromise, Hillary had accepted his decision. She had lost a battle but not the whole war. What she wrestled with was an issue of personal integrity. "Just Pretend" meant as much to her as anything else she had ever experienced. Much more to her than the sporty new Pontiac her father had bought her for her sixteenth birthday. More to her than all her fashionable clothes. More to her than any boy she had ever met or dated. She vowed to get her show—*her* show—back on the air one day soon, but for the moment the issue of Saturday's caller dominated her attention.

That and the rush of traffic into the Atlanta airport where her father would be expecting her to pick him up. He had phoned that morning to say he would be flying in from Chicago but would arrive too late for the final day's run of Dixie Excursions back to Foxpath. Normally, in similar situations, Hillary's mother would have performed taxi duty; Hillary volunteered instead—she didn't trust her mother to be sober enough to be on the road.

For Hillary, it was her first time driving in Atlanta traffic alone. First time in the airport labyrinth alone. She considered it a challenge. Like the challenge of finding the little girl whose call had spelled the end of "Just Pretend."

I pretended a bad man . . .

She had told herself a thousand times in the last few days that the key word in that call was "pretend."

Just pretend.

But no amount of rationalizing—and no amount of shopping—could keep a terrifying spectre from rising in her thoughts like the summer morning mist rising ghost-like from the surface of Foxpath Lake.

Who is she?

Hillary tried to imagine the little girl's face. She replayed the tone of her frightened voice for clues. But there was nothing. An invisible girl. A shadow.

If anything happens to that little girl . . .

It was an "if" she couldn't bear to consider.

An hour later she greeted her father with a hug as he trudged out of the exit tunnel, pale and drawn, carrying a briefcase which appeared to weigh far more than he did.

"Good trip?" she whispered.

"Got here in one piece," he said. "And so did you. Was getting into the airport a rite of passage for you?"

"It wasn't too bad," she lied.

"Then I can relax while you chauffeur me home, right?"

"I wouldn't relax too much," she said. "Traffic sorta has to make room for my maneuvers—I can promise you an exciting ride, but maybe not the most relaxing."

She surprised herself by wending her way from the airport with a minimum of confusion and wrong turns and only a handful of directions and suggestions from her father. Out on Interstate 85, the bright lights of Atlanta suburbs burning in the rearview mirror, she loosened her talonlike grip on the steering wheel and concentrated on her father's account of a successful consulting venture.

Despite the flush of success, he seemed older to Hillary than he had ever seemed before. And not just because of the sprinkling of gray in his hair and the additional crow's feet fanning out from his eyes. He was a battle-weary warrior, and she did not know his adversary, though she envisioned it as some faceless, virtually invisible force rather like . . . rather like a pretended bad man.

"Enough about this old guy's business trip," he said, perhaps sensing that she wasn't listening carefully. "What's been going on in your world?"

A nightmare.

That's how she wanted to respond.

She wanted to describe how her radio show had been yanked off the air; she wanted to share what she was feeling about the little girl who had called.

But Tucker Garrett doesn't really care about my world.

Was she being fair?

Perhaps it wasn't that he didn't care about her world as much as he simply didn't have *time* for her world.

"It's pretty quiet in my world," she said.

At first the lie was uncomfortable. Rather like swallowing a big drink of sour milk. Then it got easier—tasted better?—as she rambled on about the dates she had gone on, describing the two thoroughly forgettable boys she had been dating, about playing tennis and shopping, and about taking her sailboat out on the lake.

Nothing about "Just Pretend."

She was disappointed when her father failed to ask about the show, so she opted for a strategy that would force him to attend to her concerns.

"I'm worried about Mom," she said.

She waited as he pulled within himself before saying, "You're wasting your time. No amount of worry's going to help that woman."

That woman?

She hated the cold, detached tone of his observation.

"Her drinking's worse," said Hillary. "Can't we do something?"

"I'll speak to her if you like."

If I like?

"I think she needs our help," Hillary followed.

Through the muted glow of the dashboard lights, her father glanced over at her more than mildly irritated. He said nothing further, and within the next thirty miles he fell asleep.

At home she said good night to her father and went to her room. In a purely reflexive action, she checked her answering machine and found one message: "Hillary, this is Dave Tanner. Call me at 555-9028. This is, uh . . . very important."

Although it was after midnight, Tanner answered on the second ring.

"I knew you'd been in Atlanta today, so you might not have heard the news," he said.

"What news is that?"

"About what happened up at the lake . . . up at the old gold mine."

She waited. Something in his voice pressed at her throat. She coughed nervously and said, "Dave, are you going to tell me or do I have to guess?"

She didn't mind letting her annoyance seep into her words.

"Okay, sure. But, you know, you maybe better brace yourself, okay? It's strange news, and I think I have an idea how this is going to hit you so . . ."

"Dave!"

"Okay, sorry. Here it is." She heard him sigh, heard the rush of his breath, and it scared her. "At the mine they found . . . it was a little girl. They found the body of a little girl, and what I heard was . . . well, she'd been strangled. Probably happened over the weekend is what they think."

Hillary opened her mouth. She swallowed. But it was as if she had suddenly forgotten how to speak. Tanner's tongue clicked.

"You still there? Hillary . . . hey, I knew this would hit you . . . hey, I wish to hell you'd say something."

There was more silence.

She was trembling.

"Good night, Dave," is all she managed to say.

She lowered the receiver.

And then the night crashed around her.

Six

The lake was down.

A rainless May and a nearly rainless June had lowered the level a foot or more, and thus Clay had to wade through a soft, muddy sand beyond the derelict, weathered dock to get to the small boat.

His father's boat.

Clay now thought of it as his boat, a flat-bottomed aluminum skiff painted green, the paint peeling and chipped. The dock where it was tied had once belonged to an elderly Chinese man who had tried unsuccessfully to have a boat repair business. His corrugated tin garage stood empty; kudzu vines eyed it hungrily, and Clay had heard that the managers of "Foxtails," a camp for handicapped kids which was located adjacent to the property, were interested in acquiring it. Clay dreamed one day of splashing onto the commercial fiction market and buying the property himself.

For the moment, however, there was something else on his mind. Through the quiet dawn, through the veil of mist which hovered near the surface of the lake, he poled the skiff some two hundred yards to a secret landing where the pines thickened, the woods deepened, and outcroppings of rock loomed like prehistoric creatures.

Clay was being drawn to the site of the murder.

What did he expect to find?

He wasn't certain.

He thought again of Molly's question about possibly using his wild talent to help catch the killer.

No, I couldn't do that.

Just thinking about the potential strain of exercising his peculiar power to that extent was enough to give him a headache. And yet, there he was, tying up the skiff, sneaking through the underbrush within fifty yards of the main shaft of the old gold mine, now simply a deserted cave.

The hand of death had visited this area.

A monster had stalked its prey here.

Within twenty yards of one of the three caves, he stopped and glanced up at a forty-five degree angle to his right. A yellow ribbon cordoned off the entrance to the cave. Black lettering on the ribbon read, "Do Not Enter. Crime Investigation."

So that means it's real, Clay thought to himself. *It really happened.*

He approached cautiously, tentatively—almost as if the body of the little girl were still there, as if he somehow knew it would be there, and he had been chosen as the one to discover it.

He stopped again, this time within fifteen feet of the ribbon. As usual, the air near the caves was a bit cooler than the rest of the area; inside the caves it would be significantly cooler.

It's not the same place.

That was his thought as he surveyed where the rock of the cave spilled out onto the pinestraw and red clay floor of the woods. It was no longer a serene place, no longer the place where he and Molly would bring a brown bag lunch and explore and imagine and dream. One day they pretended that one of their ventures had led to the rediscovery of gold in the cave; afterward they had spent more than an hour tossing back and forth plans for how they would use the money.

Molly wanted to take a trip to Hollywood.

Clay wanted to buy property on the lake and build an impressive lakeside cabin to serve as his writer's retreat. And they agreed to buy an expensive car and drive to wherever The Grateful Dead happened to be in concert. And they would move their mother into a new house. And maybe they would encourage their father to stay home.

Pleasant dreams in a pleasant setting.

Now a setting where a nightmare had unfolded.

Clay took a deep breath and hunkered down near the ribbon. Hesitating several seconds, he reached out to touch a spot where the pinestraw had been disturbed and, to his momentary relief, he saw, on his powerful inner screen . . . nothing.

Then he closed his eyes.

Why am I doing this?

No, he wouldn't concentrate fully. Just reach out ever so slightly with his mind. Just a peek. Just a peek at the horror. He gritted his teeth and waited. Then opened the lens of his mind.

When the flash occurred, it dizzied him; he collapsed to one side and felt vomit push up into the back of his mouth. He coughed and spit; on his hands and knees, he tried to steady himself. Sweat beaded heavily on his forehead. The roar in his ears was as loud as a jet.

Minutes passed.

On unsteady legs, he got to his feet.

The flash which had filled his mind had been a collage of images but nothing very distinct. Nothing, he reasoned, which could aid the police. Nothing, in fact, which made much sense.

He had seen a man's hands. Or a boy's. Small hands. He had heard a gurgle—something like water going down a drain or the sound of someone being strangled. And, finally, he had seen a shadow, a shadow the size of a child, rise seemingly from the ground at the entrance to the cave and then dissipate suddenly like motes of dust scattered by a breeze, and the flash had left him with the taste of a copper penny in his mouth and a burning sensation, for no more than a second or two, on his face and hands.

Should I tell Molly about this?

Still shaken from the experience, he gave himself some distance from the cave. His breathing gradually returned to normal; the pain in his head subsided a bit.

The morning humidity began to press upon him.

And that's when he sensed that he was being watched.

Hillary spent the morning after her conversation with Dave Tanner talking with anyone at the Foxpath Police Department who might be willing to share any information they had on the murder. They weren't much help. From the *Foxpath News* she learned that the murdered girl's name was Leigh Rybeck, whose parents lived near the lake. They had reported her missing Saturday afternoon. Leigh was nine and had been accustomed to roaming the lakefront area alone and with her friends.

Determined to learn more, Hillary turned to one other

potential source of information: the district attorney for Foxpath County, a friend of her father's, an immensely capable man who, like her, loved cats. But he was forced to apologize, explaining that the investigation was locked in the slow-motion preliminary stage. He assured her, however, that if he uncovered anything he could share, he would.

During the afternoon, Hillary skulked about her parents' home on the lake in a terrible mood. Her mother told her not to look like such a sourpuss, and her father merely assumed that she was having her period. Charmian stayed near, not too close, but close enough to remind her that if she needed a sympathetic ear, she had one.

I have to ask Leigh's parents something.

That something was whether Leigh had been listening to "Just Pretend" on Saturday morning. Hillary failed in her attempt to find out. The Rybecks were not available for such questions. Hillary understood.

And so she sat on the sofa and stared at the phone, helpless, frustrated, and confused. And frightened. Very, very frightened. A murder had been committed at the old gold mine—it seemed impossible.

And the victim might have been calling her for help.

Hillary felt sick.

It felt like suffering from some terrible strain of emotional flu. Her body ached. Her heart ached. She continued to stare at the phone as if daring it to provide her with an idea of what she should do.

Then something quite strange occurred.

The phone rang.

* * *

It was a little girl's voice.

At first, Hillary believed she was hearing a ghost. She believed that last Saturday's caller was on the line, that the caller, from the realm of the supernatural, had reached out to her—but why? What could such a ghost want? Could it demand that Hillary seek out the murderer? Would it provide clues to the identity of the murderer?

But then, no, Hillary realized quickly that it wasn't a ghost.

"Who is this?" she asked, sensing a certain hesitation on the caller's part.

"My name is Molly Ann Brannon, and you don't know me, but I listen to your radio show—you know, 'Just Pretend'—and . . ."

No, dear God, not another one.

Hillary held steady as the girl fumbled to continue.

"And, you see, I'm Clay Brannon's sister, and I'm really sorry to bother you and all. I called the radio station, and they gave me your parents' number. I hope it's okay to call you."

"Yes. Yes, it's fine. Is there something you want, Molly?"

"Well, yeah. But it's kinda hard to describe. Well, okay, see what happened was, my brother and I listened to your show last Saturday and we heard that girl call, the one who said she pretended a bad man and now, well, we heard about the girl who was strangled up at the lake."

There was a long pause during which Hillary scrambled mentally to place the name: *Brannon. Clay Brannon.* It sounded vaguely familiar.

"Do you have some information about the murder?"

"Not exactly. But kinda, yeah. Do you know my brother

Clay? He goes to Foxpath High, too, and he knows you. He's a real good writer."

Yes, suddenly Hillary recalled a young man with long black hair and a sensitive, rather handsome face who had genuine creative ability. While she hadn't really ever talked with him or gotten to know him, she did have a favorable impression.

"I've had a class with him, I'm pretty sure."

"Well, he can help catch the killer."

Stunned by the girl's comment, Hillary twisted the phone cord. She had no clear sense of where the girl was headed with her comments.

"Molly, if your brother has information about this case, he should go to the police. I appreciate the fact that you would call me, but the police should be given any information you have on this matter."

"No, it's not like that. My brother doesn't really have information. What he's got is . . . he can *see* things."

"What do you mean?"

"It's kinda weird, but he really can do it. He can see who's been in a room when they're not there no more. There's a science kind of word for it—an 'imaging' ability. I don't remember the big word. Doctors say he doesn't really have it, but he does. It makes him pretty sick to do it."

Bits and pieces of rumor floated down the stream of Hillary's memory. Yes, she recalled hearing something about Clay Brannon having such an ability. And yet, she had given it little credence. It seemed to fit in the category of curious high school gossip.

"I'm confused, Molly. Shouldn't you and your brother be talking with the police instead of me?"

"The thing is . . . Clay, he won't tell the police he can do this. But I thought maybe he would if *you* asked him. I thought you'd maybe be pretty upset about the murder and maybe you could talk to Clay and ask him to help you catch the killer."

"I am concerned," said Hillary. "Yes, of course. But I don't know your brother very well at all, and it still seems to me that he should get in touch with the police. Don't you think that would be best?"

There was disappointment in Molly's tone when she finally responded.

"Well, I guess so. Maybe it would. I probably shouldn't oughtta called you. I'm sorry."

"No, Molly, it's fine. Honey, I'm glad you did. But if your brother can help with the investigation, I really believe he should contact the police or sheriff's department or even the district attorney's office."

Molly reluctantly agreed, then said good-bye and hung up.

Her curiosity pricked, Hillary punched in the number of her friend Robin Clawson.

"Robin, this is Hillary."

"Hey, Hillie, what you up to?"

Robin, a strikingly attractive young woman, delivered her every comment in an overly friendly, overly eager tone. She and Hillary weren't close friends, but they had been on the cheerleader squad together and had double-dated a few times. Robin could be downright annoying, a bit too much of an airhead—and beyond that, Hillary despised being called "Hillie."

"I need some guy stuff."

"Oh-o-o, now you've got my attention."

"What can you tell me about Clay Brannon?"

"Hmm, well . . . he's cute. That's obvious. And smart. Too smart maybe. His folks don't have much money. I think maybe his dad left the family. I'm not sure. Clay's not dating anyone as far as I know. Why, you interested? Are you going to give him a call?"

"Probably not. It's a rather involved story. His younger sister, Molly, just phoned and—"

"You know about her, don't you? About Molly?"

For a second or two Hillary experienced a roaring in her ears. She had no idea what to anticipate, but it was clear that Robin was either about to shed some light on an evolving mystery or darken it significantly. Or both.

"No. Nothing much except that she listens to my radio show. She sounds like a smart little kid over the phone."

"She's dying."

"What?"

"Yeah, she's got some kind of cancer, and what I've heard is that she's pretty sick and they don't think, you know, she'll make it. That's just what I've heard."

"No. No, I wasn't aware of that."

Finding it suddenly difficult to swallow, Hillary thanked Robin for her information, cutting off the other young woman's bubbly eagerness.

It was nearing dark by the time Hillary reached the area of the old gold mine. She had a flashlight with her, but she carried it at her side as one might an unloaded gun.

What am I doing here?

Curiosity had pulled her.

And something more: she had needed to get away from

the house, away from her parents who had launched into a pointless argument at dinner.

And she had needed to think.

About Molly Brannon's call.

Common sense dictated that she not try to contact Clay Brannon. First, the murder was being investigated by the police or the sheriff's department or both, so there was no reason for any private citizen to become involved.

Unless . . .

He can see who's been in a room when they're not there no more.

Unless that private citizen really could help.

But I don't really know Clay Brannon.

Then another inner voice said, *And you never knew the little girl who was murdered.*

Murdered close by.

Hillary made her way through the underbrush, stickery bushes and limbs tearing at her jeans. It was warm and humid and still. The twilight was crouched and hushed.

She climbed until she reached the yellow ribbon strung along in front of the cave. For a perverse moment, she was reminded of an old song entitled "Tie a Yellow Ribbon." But this yellow ribbon had no romantic overtones. This yellow ribbon meant death.

She's dying.

That's what Robin had said about Molly Brannon.

What a terrible, terrible thing.

A little girl dying. A little girl concerned about the murder of someone possibly very much like herself. Hillary suddenly realized that she wanted to meet Molly Brannon.

Somehow, in that ghostly twilight, standing near the opening of the cave, standing so close to where a little girl had been murdered—*possibly* the same little girl who had called her show—Hillary sensed a curious connection between that girl and Molly Brannon.

It was as if the shadows of the two girls had merged.

And Hillary had witnessed it.

With darkness gathering, she decided to switch on her flashlight and go home; she had walked the entire distance from her parents' house rather than boat to the area. The exercise had felt good, but now the thought of the long walk made her feel tired.

Scanning the mouth of the cave with the beam of light, she saw nothing. No visible sign that a small life had been snuffed out. She turned to go. And a voice broke through the glass of night.

"Priddy Ann?"

A man's voice.

Startled, Hillary swung the beam up and to her right just beyond the cave opening.

"Priddy Ann? Is that you?"

The beam momentarily captured the amber eyes of a man with a heavy beard.

Hillary stared.

And then she screamed.

And as she began to run, she dropped the flashlight; terrified, she thrashed her way wildly through the dark woods, expecting, at every heartbeat, for the man behind the voice to chase her down.

Seven

"You look like you're 'bout to turn and run."

The thin, pale girl in the bed forced a smile at the end of that observation; Hillary felt a flush of embarrassment.

"Oh, Molly, I'm sorry. No, I'm not planning to run. In fact, I'm very glad to meet you. I wasn't sure they were going to let me visit you this afternoon."

Crooking a finger conspiratorially, Molly gestured for Hillary to come closer.

"I told 'em this big story 'bout how you were my cousin and I hadn't seen you for years and it was sorta like a last wish to get to see you again before they pulled the sheet up over my head and you know what? They fell for it. Sometimes, you know, it's fun to break the rules."

It was Hillary's turn to smile. She was delighted with Molly Brannon. Her mischievousness. Her warmth. Her courage.

"You mean like my not wearing my hospital mask? Are you sure that's okay?"

"Yeah, my brother never wears his unless a nurse is around. The way I figure it, what difference does it make? My sparkler's burning down anyway. And I can't understand what people are saying when they have on a mask."

"You know, Molly, I've got to be honest. I was apprehensive about coming here, and I'm still not certain I've done the right thing, but, like I've said, I wanted to meet you."

Too weak to smile broadly, Molly nodded. There were dark circles under her eyes. In the last day or so, she had lost ground. Her doctor feared some internal bleeding, perhaps bladder and urinary tract.

"Most people don't much like coming into a leukie's room. I guess 'cause they think maybe they'll get what we got. But you won't and—hey, can I tell you something?"

"Sure. Go ahead."

"You're really pretty. When I listen to your show, I try to imagine what you look like. I didn't know you're so pretty. Does my brother Clay know how pretty you are?"

Hillary put her fingers to her lips to stifle a chuckle.

"Why, thanks for the compliment, Molly. And as far as your brother is concerned, I don't believe he knows much about me period. Nor do I know much about him."

"He's really a super neat guy. He thinks I'm pretty even though I lost all my hair." She paused a moment and studied Hillary's hair. "Hey, how do you think you'd look bald like me?"

"Oh, dear. Some days, when my hair has a mind of its own, I think I'd be better off without it."

"Yeah, us girls have to worry too much 'bout hair. Isn't that so?"

"I agree one hundred percent. I'm glad my show is—or I should say 'was'—on radio, so I haven't had to worry about my appearance."

Molly shook her head as if perplexed. When she frowned, silken wrinkles inched into the paleness of her scalp.

"Do you mean you're not doin' your show no more? That'd be a real bummer. Don't say you're not doin' your show. Please."

"I'm afraid that's the situation. The station manager had to take it off the air. I won't be on this coming Saturday, and maybe not ever again."

"But why? Clay and I really like your show."

Deciding to be completely honest with Molly, Hillary launched into a step by step account of the matter, concluding by saying, "I could have compromised. I could have cut that one segment, but it just didn't feel right."

"I'm on your side," said Molly. "You did the right thing. It wasn't your fault that one girl called. They shouldn't blame you. I thought the 'pretending' was the best part of your show. My favorite part."

Hillary brightened.

"What do you pretend?" she asked. Then, almost immediately, she wondered whether she had posed the worst possible question for that context. Wasn't the answer obvious? Wouldn't Molly say that she liked to pretend she was healthy? That she liked to pretend she was like any other little girl who would grow up and be whatever she wanted to be? Would the question make her feel uncomfortable?

It didn't.

"Neat stuff. One thing I always pretend is being a movie actress, you know, a girl actress like Drew Barrymore was in *Firestarter*. Only now, she's not a girl no more. She does grown-up parts, but I'm still a kid, so I'd play kid parts. I'd like to be in a horror movie or maybe a movie that Steven Spielberg did, you know, like *E.T.* I pretend I make lots of money, and I pretend Clay writes movie stories just for me and I get to be real, real good at acting and win an Academy Award and get to make a speech and thank people."

"Who would you thank?"

"Mostly Clay."

"You obviously think very highly of him."

"Yeah, well, I do. He visits me every day, and we used to do all kinds of things together, especially up at the lake. We'd go fishing and swimming and lots of times we'd go to the old gold mine and just hang out, you know, or have a picnic."

The mention of the gold mine touched Hillary like an icy finger.

"I visited that gold mine last night and I'm still trying to get over what happened."

"Did you see where that girl got killed?"

"Yes. At least I saw where the police had marked off an area; I assume that's where the murder occurred. I had no business going to see it—I was just . . . curious. And I felt guilty."

"Guilty? Like, you mean, a guilty conscience? Why?"

"Because . . . I'm not sure exactly. It's just that if the girl who called my show is the same girl who was murdered, I feel sort of . . . responsible. And I feel like I should have been able to help."

"How? How could you have helped?"

Hillary shook her head and shrugged.

"I don't know. I asked the sheriff's department to find out if the parents knew if their daughter listened to my show and if she had called Saturday morning. Apparently they didn't know one way or the other. So . . . I feel so in the dark. And when I was at the gold mine, I saw this man."

After she described the man to Molly, the girl flashed a knowing grin.

"Don't you know the 'Foxpath Fiend?' "

Hillary thought a moment.

"That name sounds familiar. This morning I told the sheriff's department about him, and they said they'd check it out. Tell me what you know about this person you think I saw."

"Oh, it's him. He's kind of crazy, I guess," Molly began, and then recited all that she and Clay and most of the other residents in the area of Foxpath Lake knew about him.

"Do you think he's a suspect?"

"Could be. Maybe."

"I haven't been so frightened in a long, long time. I thought for certain he was coming after me, but when I stopped running and looked over my shoulder, he was nowhere in sight."

Visibly tired, Molly sank deeper into a pillow against which she was propped. Her eyes, however, held a gleam.

"Whoever did it, whoever killed that girl, I sure hope they catch him."

"I do, too." Hillary hesitated a moment and then added, "I've been thinking about what you said, what you said about Clay and how perhaps he could help. I'm frustrated because the police and the sheriff don't seem to have any leads. Almost no clues. Molly, do you really believe Clay could do something that would make a difference in the case?"

"Yeah. I'm not makin' stuff up, I promise. He can. I know he can."

"Do you think I should talk to him?"

For an instant, but only an instant, something flickered across Molly's face—a light. Something like the winking of a light on a Christmas tree.

"Yeah, I really do. And I can tell you where you can probably find him. I know where you can probably find him before he goes to work. He works at Kroger's, but I bet I know where he'll be before he has to go to work. I'll tell you because I like you. I want you to be my friend. I think you're pretty cool."

Hillary felt a smile mushrooming from her stomach.

"And *I* think *you're* pretty cool. So . . . tell me where I can locate this 'super neat guy,' your brother."

And Molly did.

On the drive back to the lake, Hillary thought she knew what a miner must feel like when he's struck a vein of ore—the thrill of a valuable discovery, the exhilaration of expected wealth.

For Hillary, it was not a monetary gain. It was something for the heart, not for the purse or bank account. She had discovered a wonderful little human being. A bright, warm, and courageous soul. A friend.

Hillary felt lucky.

And she wished that she had known Molly Brannon longer, and she silently prayed that she *would* get to know the girl longer, for it was difficult to put aside the obvious: Molly Brannon was a very sick child.

But not too sick to give of herself.

Hillary glanced at her rearview mirror. There, hanging on a chain of tiny, colorful beads, was a gift that Molly had offered her before she left the hospital. A necklace with a pendant shaped like a small, red heart, and if one looked closely one could see that the heart had a miniscule break in it, and across the break a miniscule Band-Aid.

"The whole world," Molly explained, "has got a broken heart. Maybe love won't heal it, but it's a pretty good Band-Aid. You keep this with you for luck and to remember the day you visited me, okay?"

Emotion had welled into Hillary's throat. She had thanked her new friend and said, "Molly . . . you're somebody I'll never ever forget."

And the girl had whispered, "That's cool. Hope you find Clay."

Hillary hoped so, too.

Not far from the lake, she spotted the area Molly had described. She pulled over onto the shoulder, and when she looked into the tall grass and the thicket bordering the area, she saw a bicycle leaning against a gravestone.

This must be it.

The Children's Graveyard.

Like the gold mine, this was an area Hillary had heard about but not frequented. She felt like a stranger in a strange land as she pressed through the warm afternoon air into the unkempt cemetery.

I feel like a trespasser.

This is their place. Clay's and Molly's.

What would she find here? What would she say to Molly's brother?

She walked deeper among the graves, hesitating occasionally to stoop over and read the engravings. At one point, she experienced a slight shiver when she imagined running into the man she had seen at the gold mine.

What had Molly called him?

Oh, yes, the Foxpath Fiend.

She decided that she should let Clay know she was there, but before she could shatter the silence with his name, someone behind her said, "Shiver and quiver, little tree,/Silver and gold throw down over me."

Hillary wheeled around to meet Clay Brannon's inquiring eyes and the suggestion of a smile—the very same type of smile she had seen playing at the corners of Molly Brannon's mouth.

The exchange of introductions was awkward, and yet some of the uneasiness was diminished because they had seen each other at school and because they had had at least one class together.

Clay directed her to a shady spot under a sweet gum, and they sat and Clay asked, "Haven't ever seen you here. Do you come around very often?"

"No. This is my first time. From the road it's hard to tell there's anything like this. No, I came because I was looking for you."

"Me? I don't get it."

She debated the color of his eyes—brown or hazel or a shade of green she had never encountered? He was more handsome than she had recalled. Slightly taller, as well. Sensitive. That was the word which came to mind. His long black hair looked clean. She smiled to herself at the sight of chin stubble and the peace symbol earring. But they seemed to fit. Everything about him seemed to fit.

She felt the tug of attraction, but then forced herself to concentrate on what had brought her to the graveyard.

"I need to talk with you."

"Wait—how did you know where I'd be?"

Hillary smiled.

"Molly," she said.

Clay rolled his eyes and looked away momentarily, and when he turned back he was nodding as if suddenly everything had become perfectly clear.

"Hmm, I see. My dear, sweet little sister. Let me see if I can put together the pieces of this: she called you, right? And this has something to do with your show and the little girl who called . . . and now, the murder, and—"

"She's remarkable," Hillary interjected. "Molly is absolutely remarkable. I spent less than an hour with her earlier, but in that time she stole my heart."

"Yeah . . . she's good at that."

"She's crazy about you. Worships you, in fact."

Clay looked away again. Hillary sensed that the silence which closed around him was the silence of the unsayable. That the mere mention of the name "Molly" transported him into a realm in which language fails.

She saw him blink away the emotion of the moment.

"She, uh . . . she's a great kid. A guy couldn't ask for a better sister. She and I, we've always been, you know, pretty close, but when she got sick it was like she became part of me, like when you graft a limb onto a sapling . . . do you understand what I mean?"

"Yes. I think so. A special bond. Oh, that sounds too trite. But, yes, now that I've met her and now, talking with you, I can believe you two have an unusually close relationship."

"We used to come here all the time," he followed. "It seems ironic to me, you know. It was as if we were *drawn* here. Drawn to this cemetery, but it's not an ordinary cemetery. I mean, well, in case you haven't noticed, almost every grave is the grave of a child. So many of them died at about the same time—around the turn of the century. Maybe from a yellow fever epidemic. That's just a theory I have. But, anyway, children and death—neither one of us knew that Molly would soon be facing death."

Hillary surveyed the dejection in his face; she drank in the sadness filling his eyes.

"It doesn't make her blink," she said. "She doesn't appear to be depressed or anything like that. She doesn't appear to feel sorry for herself. I admire that. And her concern for the girl who called my show . . . and the girl who was murdered—it's heartfelt and genuine."

Clay agreed.

And then he said, "Do you think they're the same? Two girls? Or one?"

"I have no way of knowing for certain. If it's a coincidence, it's an incredible coincidence. I've talked with the police and the sheriff's department and they haven't been able to help much. Frankly, I don't have much confidence in them. I'm frustrated. Molly's call offered some hope, and so here I am."

It seemed to Hillary that Clay deliberately kept the conversation focused on the murder and away from his possible involvement in solving the case. She told him about her encounter at the gold mine with the man Molly believed was the Foxpath Fiend; Clay seconded his sister's opinion.

When they could dance around the issue no longer, Clay

said, "Look, I know what you want to ask and the answer is 'no.' Regardless of what Molly may have told you, I just can't help."

"But why not? If what Molly says about your talent or ability or whatever it should be called is true, then why not use it? Are you afraid the authorities won't believe you?"

"Do you believe I can do what Molly says?"

His question caught her like an unexpected punch.

"I . . . I'm not sure. But I wish you wouldn't say no before you think about it some more."

She really didn't see it coming. His anger. The sudden rise of fury. The look in his eyes. A look of disgust for her.

"You're not used to being told no, are you? I imagine your parents never said no to you. You've probably had everything you've ever asked for. Well, this time, you can't. This time you won't get your way. The answer is 'no.' I won't help you."

His words stung her. The sudden shift in their exchange sent her reeling.

"You don't think I'm sincere about this, do you?" she shot back. Her cheeks burned. Her throat narrowed. She blinked at needle pricks of tears in the corners of her eyes. "This isn't some game. A little girl's been murdered, and I'm asking you to help because your sister claims that you might be able to—it has nothing to do with my parents or whether I'm used to getting my way."

He had pushed to his feet before she finished; he grabbed his bike, and as he swung past her he exclaimed, "The answer's 'no!' And another thing—stay away from Molly!"

Eight

"Shiver and quiver, little tree,/Silver and gold throw down over me."

Molly recited the words in a reverent, yet singsong rhythm, the kind of rhythm that only a child can render convincingly. To Clay, she made the words sound mystical. Holy.

It was the morning after his conversation with Hillary Garrett, and part of him continued to fume over her request. And part of him wanted to be angry at Molly for suggesting that Hillary ask what she did. He had come to Molly's hospital room, having rehearsed a speech in which he would severely scold his sister.

Twenty minutes into his visit, the speech remained unspoken.

"Cabby? What's that come from? Is that something you made up? You know, the 'shiver and quiver' saying. What's it come from?"

The nurse on duty had told Clay that Molly had had a rough night. Dr. Winston had confirmed that she was, indeed, experiencing some internal bleeding, but he believed he could get it under control. And this morning, she seemed perkier, though a ghostly sheen masked her face. Clay had come with his mother earlier that morning, and she had spent some time with Molly alone. And now the woman waited in the cafeteria downstairs—the visit had visibly upset her. Clay doubted that it had been of much value for Molly, either.

"It's from a real old version of *Cinderella*. It's a ritualistic wish," he explained.

Molly patted her hands together very softly. There was a smile in her eyes born of a pleasant memory.

"We used to make that wish in the Children's Graveyard. Do you remember? You told me the graveyard would be a lucky place to wish for something because the souls of all those kids would sorta team up and help an alive kid get their wish—boy howdy, you could really bullshit me when I was younger."

Clay chuckled.

"You got a trashy mouth, little sister, you know that?"

"It's from bein' around all the other leukies. They cuss every other word, you know. Especially Bradley. But he doesn't do it when grown-ups are in the room. Bradley's such a pissant."

"He been stealing any more chocolate from you?"

Molly shook her head enthusiastically.

"Nope. He's 'fraid to. I threatened to tell the nurses he's got copies of *Playboy* stashed in his coat closet."

Burying her head deeper in her pillow, Molly fought to keep her eyes open. She spider-walked one hand out over the top of the sheet, seeking out Clay's hand. He covered hers with his and said, "How you feeling?"

She looked at him and grinned.

"Well, I think I'll skip my ten-mile run this afternoon if you don't mind."

He had to smile at that one. And then he said, "Seriously. How are you?"

She stiffened her chin, but he saw her lips quiver; she squeezed her eyes shut tightly and whispered, "Just hold my hand, okay?"

And so he did.

They let several minutes pass in silence. Brother and sister. Hand in hand. The room filled with their closeness. And then Clay began to hum an old Beatles' tune—"Let It Be"—and Molly smiled.

After another minute, he stopped humming.

"How'd your visit with Mom go?" he asked. He hadn't forgotten about his plan to scold his sister for her behind-the-scenes maneuvering, and he wasn't exactly avoiding sharing what had taken place between him and Hillary Garrett. He just wanted to feel the pulse of Molly's emotions.

"Not too bad, 'cept she used up all my Kleenex. Really, she was doin' pretty good 'til I asked her if she could find Dad and have him come see me 'cause I don't know how much time . . . and she just freaked, you know, and, well, it's probably her last visit, and that's okay."

"It'd been better not to say anything about Dad. I mean, what's the point? Why would you want to see him anyway? He walked out on us—walked out on you especially."

Molly's shrug was barely perceptible.

"I guess just 'cause . . . 'cause he's my dad. Your dad, too. The only dad we got. Maybe if she told him I wanted to see him, he would come."

"Don't count on it, Molly. Don't count on ever seeing him."

Molly rolled her head to one side and then let it roll weakly back so that she was focused once again on Clay.

"I feel like I wanna hear a story. Would you read to me?"

"You got it. What you want to hear?"

"About the girl who sailed away—you got any more of that story written?"

He nodded.

"Some. Rough draft. Don't you want to wait till I can polish the whole piece?"

"No. I don't think maybe I better *wait* for anything— read it from the beginning. I'm gonna close my eyes and see the story in my mind. Just like a little movie."

Clay got out his notebook. It never ceased to amaze him how calming it was to have it in his hands. And reading to Molly was like being connected to her with a thousand invisible threads.

He cleared his throat and began.

"This is a story about the girl who sailed away on a sea no one else had ever sailed. She sailed away because she had to. It was time for her to do so. And no one else had ever sailed upon that sea because there was no one else like this particular girl. That sea existed only for her. A sea of her very own. And she had built a special boat for her voyage, a boat like no one else's. And she had set sail at night because she liked the night. And she was not concerned that she might lose her way because she was guided by the stars.

"Besides, you see, the girl who sailed away did not know her destination. Nor did she need to. It was that kind of voyage."

Pausing, Clay glanced up.

Molly's face had relaxed; she was asleep. And she was snoring softly.

Not exactly a story that keeps somebody on the edge of their seat, he mused.

He went over to Molly and, as he often did, leaned down and kissed her on the forehead. It felt unusually warm and he wondered whether he should ring for a nurse. He decided to let Molly sleep, to let her sail away on a sea of dreams and be oblivious to—for a few minutes at least—the ugly shore of reality.

When, within the next half an hour, she woke, she said, "I dreamed about you and Hillary."

"Oh, come on. You didn't."

"Yeah, and you know what happened in the dream?"

"No, and I really don't want to know either."

Molly stuck out her tongue at him.

"You gotta hear it, or it won't come true. See, what I dreamed was this: you and Hillary had to climb down into this big, dark box . . . and I think you were trying to save someone. I think there was somebody crying. Maybe a kid. Wasn't that a weird dream?"

"Sounds like you made it up because you want me and Hillary to hit it off."

"She's hot-lookin', right? You like her, don't you?"

"No, not particularly. She's a rich kid who's used to having people give her what she wants. And if she can't get someone to do her a favor, she'll buy the favor."

"Wow, did she offer you money yesterday? What happened?"

Clay conjured up the meanest, most penetrating glare he could.

"You know what happened—*you* were pulling the strings all the way."

Molly looked nonplussed. Or pretended to.

"Oh, come on, Molly. Are you going to tell me you didn't encourage Hillary to ask me to get involved with that little girl's murder case?"

"All's I told her was the truth: you could maybe identify the killer."

"Maybe. But probably not. Probably I would get in the way. Probably the people investigating the case would tell me to get the hell out."

Clay could see that Molly was going to pout.

"Look," he added, "I'm gonna go get a can of soda. You want anything?"

She shook her head.

When Clay returned, he didn't see it coming until it was too late.

The lake that evening was breathtakingly beautiful.

Lost in thought and only partially aware of that beauty, Clay poled his father's skiff in the waters not far from the old gold mine. But he was not preoccupied with the mine or the recent murder there or with the Foxpath Fiend as a possible suspect; likewise, he gave no concentrated thought to Hillary Garrett.

Lodged in his mental filter was Molly's voice.

The inner screen of his thought was dominated by her face.

Just before he had left her hospital room that afternoon they had been listening to some Hendrix and to some of The Doors; they had laughed a little, especially at Bradley scurrying from room to room, attempting to find a new hiding place for his *Playboy* magazines.

And then Clay had said, "Got a time clock to punch, Queen Mab. Kroger calls."

"I need another minute," Molly had responded.

Her face took on a flat look of seriousness, like freshly cleaned glass. A face reaching for a point of clarity.

"Your IV need changing?"

"No. Nothing like that."

He was wary of her tone.

"What is it, then?"

"I gotta ask you something. Gotta ask you to do something for me."

"Molly, you know I'd do anything in the world for you."

She appeared to want to milk the moment to the fullest. She glanced at the ceiling; she bit her lip; she folded her small hands together as if in prayer.

"I want you to promise me something," she said.

The rush of apprehension Clay had felt came back to him there on the lake with the moon, no longer a full moon, sending down a muted shower of light.

"Molly," he had said, "if it's about Dad, I—"

"No. It's not about him. It's about you." She took a deep breath and then continued. "I want you to promise me you'll use your imaging ability to help catch whoever killed that little girl."

Her mouth had tightened and she had stared at him hard, and yet there had also been a pleading in those loving eyes.

"Molly, damn it, I can't—"

"Please, Cabby. For me. Promise."

And he had felt his resolve begin to melt almost instantly. He had felt like a candle burning down.

He had called in sick. He figured there was no way he

could give his undivided attention to his job in the produce department.

What haunted him as the skiff began to drift aimlessly was the simple fact that Molly had extracted from him a promise—yes, he had agreed—but all around him, with the moon as witness, shadows rose from the water. And he knew, knew in a way that he would never be able to explain to Molly or to Hillary Garrett, that his promise would place him in an extremely dangerous situation.

The next morning he brought Molly a box of Milk Duds.

She was delighted to see him and let him know so by giving him a long hug. Clay thought it was a little like being hugged by a sack of straw—she seemed so weightless. So vulnerable. And yet she maintained that she was feeling better than yesterday.

"I begged Marcie for some eyeshadow, but she wouldn't come up with it. I bet I look like a frog, don't I? I got to have some makeup on my eyes or I look like a frog. What a shitter."

Marcie was the on-duty nurse and frowned on most of Molly's ways.

"You're too young for makeup," said Clay. "Besides, you don't need it. I think you're gorgeous without it."

"Boy howdy, are you ever blind," Molly exclaimed.

But she looked pleased.

"Hey, you know, I can't stay long this morning."

"Why not?"

"Because I called in sick last night and so I need to go in today and pick up the lost hours."

"What kind of sick? Did you eat some hospital food?"

They both laughed, and Molly gestured for him to punch in a tape. He did. The Beatles and "Yesterday."

"No, I wasn't really sick."

"So why'd you call in sick?"

"I was just . . . I don't know—upset."

" 'Bout what?"

"Come on, Molly, you oughtta be able to guess."

"The promise?"

She gestured again, this time for Clay to turn down the volume.

"Look," he said, "it's just that I don't know what I'm getting myself into. I mean, it scares the hell outta me. And I don't think Hillary Garrett knows how freaky deaky things could get."

"Do you hate her guts?"

"Molly, damn it, no. No . . . I don't hate her."

"Do you think she's pretty?"

He shrugged, embarrassed. "Yeah, well, she looks good, but . . . that's not the point."

Molly touched a finger to her lips. It was a thoughtful pose.

"I wonder if Hillary likes rock 'n roll?"

"She probably likes country western—you know, Randy Travis and Garth Brooks."

Molly curled up her lip.

"O-o-o-h, I hope not. That'd be awful. That'd mean you two couldn't get married. Country western o-o-o-h, gag."

"Married? Little sister, have you flipped out? What color's the sky in your world? Man, if you think there'll ever be anything between me and—"

"Hey, Cabby, you can never tell about love."

* * *

She had seemed so upbeat when he left for Kroger's.

But when Bob Swaim, the produce manager at the store, put his hand on Clay's shoulder and said, "The Foxpath Medical Center just called. You need to get over there right away," Clay felt as if the morning high had been sucked out of him instantly, leaving an empty, raw feeling. He dropped the bunch of white grapes he was holding and tore off his plastic gloves.

His mother met him in the hallway outside the door to Molly's room.

"She took a bad turn, son. Dr. Winston said she's bleedin' inside, and there's fever, but she's resting some now, and he said if she can get through the night she'll—"

"She will, damn it. Don't say 'if'—Molly's gonna make it."

His mother reeled back from him as if she'd had hot grease spattered on her.

"All's I'm tellin' you is what Dr. Winston said. You ask him yourself. It's touch an' go. You ask him."

He pushed by her and by the on-duty nurse and didn't stop for any of the pre-visit rituals. Molly was asleep. Clay could see that she was breathing, and the sense of relief he felt almost caused his knees to buckle.

He noticed that the package of Milk Duds had not been opened.

Hold on, Molly. My Queen Mab. You gotta hold on.

He sat next to her bed and waited.

In a blue-white haze of fear, he waited.

Two hours later she woke.

"Dad here yet?" she asked in a thimble voice.

"What?"

"Mom said Dad would be here. She was pretty sure."

Clay shook his head; he couldn't keep from gritting his teeth.

"Oh, Molly, she lied to you. He's not coming."

"Why'd she say he was?"

He shook his head again.

"Maybe she thought . . . maybe she thought it would make you feel better, but you and I, we've always been honest with each other about important stuff . . . and the thing is, Dad's not coming to see you. I'm sorry."

"Well, it's okay," she said softly. " 'Cause you're here."

Moments later, she dozed off again for about half an hour. Dr. Winston and the "heme" team came as she was waking. They asked Clay to leave the room, and he did so, but reluctantly.

A score of minutes passed before Winston told him, "All we can do is wait and see. You'll want to tell your mother, I'm sure. I believe she's in the waiting room next to the chapel.

He found her there, sitting with a Bible open in her lap as if it were an empty plate, as if she had eaten but was still hungry. She didn't want to return to Molly's room, so Clay decided not to press the matter. He was disgusted with her for handing Molly a lie, and yet, seeing her there, seeing how small and pathetic she looked, he couldn't bring himself to voice that disgust.

Back in Molly's room, his sister greeted him with as much of a smile as she could muster.

"It's safe," she said. "All the ghouls and vampires are gone." She paused, then added, "Sorry I'm makin' you miss work."

"Hey, forget it. People will buy those grapes and melons whether I'm there or not. Besides, I'd much rather be here."

Her hand moved, a reflexive jerk, but she was too weak to reach out for him, so he reached for her and clasped her hand and closed his eyes.

And saw something. Felt something.

What he saw was Molly and yet not Molly.

Molly's shadow? Her ghost? No, ghosts were supposed to be pale; you could see through them like old, badly worn sheets. What he saw was dark. Shadowy. Shaped liked Molly. Like something she had left behind.

It jolted him.

"You okay?" he asked.

She could barely move her lips.

"I been better," she whispered.

"Wanna hear some Joplin or maybe some Hendrix?"

She surprised him by shaking her head.

Molly's never turned down rock 'n roll.

He swallowed hard. As he held her hand, he tried to feel a pulse. It seemed so faint.

Suddenly, Molly said, quite softly, "What happened to her?"

"Who's 'her'?"

"You know. The girl who sailed away."

"Oh, yeah . . . that girl. You wanna hear?"

She nodded.

And so he pulled a chair close to her bed and turned to the final pages of his notebook. He cleared his throat, but before he could begin, Molly said, "Cabby?"

He stood up and leaned over so that he could hear her.

"Yeah?"

He watched her lips move as if struggling to find the right shape for the words she wanted to say. He waited, and then, at last, she said, "I love you, Cabby."

When he sat back down he had no feeling in his body; he sensed only that his heart had swelled to such a size that it had swallowed his body. He looked at the words on the pages of his notebook and wasn't at all certain he could read them. He wasn't aware of just how long he stared at the pages, locked in a reverie of emotion quite unlike any other he had ever experienced.

But then he heard Molly murmur a bit impatiently, "I don't got all night."

And the reverie was broken. He smiled and said, "I love you, too, Molly. I'll always love you."

Her eyes were closed. But he could tell she was ready to listen. He took a deep breath and began.

"This is a story about the girl who sailed away on a sea no one else had ever sailed. She sailed away because she had to. It was time for her to do so. And no one else had ever sailed upon that sea because there was no one else like this particular girl. That sea existed only for her. A sea of her very own. And she had built a special boat for her voyage, a boat like no one else's. And she had set sail at night because she liked the night. And she was not concerned that she might lose her way because she was guided by the stars.

"Besides, you see, the girl who sailed away did not know her destination. Nor did she need to. It was that kind of voyage. She sailed far into the night. The stars guided her to an island where she stopped to listen to a ghostly concert. There was Hendrix and Joplin, Lennon and Jim Morrison, and someone who looked quite a lot like Elvis. She enjoyed the concert, but she sailed on. Beyond the music. Beyond the night. Beyond the stars.

"Until she reached a place of her own.

"And there she knew her voyage had ended."

Clay closed his notebook.

Aside from a nurse interrupting his vigil a few times, he sat alone at Molly's bedside and watched her sleep. He sat for an hour. Then another. He turned off all the lights except for the lamp next to the bed.

When he sensed that it was time to go, he got up and went to Molly and kissed her on the forehead and said, "Good night, Queen Mab."

He turned and walked several steps before he stopped and went to her again. This time he whispered, "Goodbye," and switched off the lamp and left the room.

At ten minutes until midnight, Molly Ann Brannon died.

Nine

Leigh Rybeck's mother had given Hillary a photo of her murdered daughter. As Hillary drove toward the Foxpath Lake Marina, she thought about that photo, knew exactly where it was in the purse on the seat beside her, and replayed a conversation she had had with Mrs. Rybeck yesterday afternoon.

"Leigh felt like the lake belonged to her," the woman had said, her eyes still puffy from a series of crying bouts she'd experienced since the news of her daughter's death, the most intense bout coming at the funeral. Hillary had attended that funeral, mostly to lend her sympathy to the Rybecks but also because she'd once heard a bizarre theory that a murderer occasionally became an observer at the graveside ritual of his victim.

But Hillary hadn't noticed any suspicious characters.

During their conversation, Mrs. Rybeck had handed Leigh's photo to Hillary and added, "I just never thought she would be in danger. She was an excellent swimmer, and so I didn't worry about her being near the lake. It always seemed like such a safe environment."

And she had glanced up at Hillary, bereft, looking to see whether Hillary agreed.

"Mrs. Rybeck, did Leigh ever mention anything to you

about *pretending* a bad man? Anything recently about being frightened of a strange man?"

The woman had paused momentarily, then had pushed several strands of strawberry-blond hair behind her ear, a seemingly unconscious gesture, giving her conscious attention to Hillary's question.

"No. No, I don't recall that kind of thing. Though once she told me and my husband that she had seen the ghost of a little girl up near the gold mine—you know, kids seeing ghosts—we didn't take it seriously."

Drawn to the innocent smile in the photo, Hillary had studied the blond-haired, blue-eyed charming countenance of Leigh Rybeck. The slight gap between her front teeth would have given the local orthodontist some business one day soon. The dimples would soon have driven little boys wild—perhaps had already.

She's missed all the joys and hungers of life, Hillary had thought to herself, and then, not entirely certain why, she had told Mrs. Rybeck of her guilt, the details of her show, including, especially, the incident of the terrified caller.

While she understood and sympathized, Marla Rybeck doubted seriously that her daughter had called.

"Only God knows what really happened," she said, "and, regardless, nothing can bring back my Leigh. I hope and pray the person who did this will be caught and punished, but nothing can change what is. Nothing can change what I feel. Except time. You shouldn't feel responsible. It's just the world. We live in a sick, ugly world. My husband and I thought we had escaped from it when we built up here on the lake. But the ugliness followed us, it seems."

And that had been the end of the conversation.

And now Hillary was determined to pursue the latest word in the official investigation of Leigh Rybeck's murder. As she parked in front of the mobile unit housing the Foxpath Lake Shore Patrol, she was not optimistic. Thus far, the law enforcement personnel assigned to the case had accomplished little more than raising the anxiety level of everyone at the lake.

She hoped her appointment with Donnie Ray Giles, a shore patrol officer, would boost her confidence in the possibility that the case would soon be closed, a killer apprehended.

"Ms. Garrett, how you been? Come right on in. This is sorta 'Command Central,' you might say. Can I get you a Coke or something?"

Hillary shook her head and said, "No, thank you." She sat in a plastic chair and quickly surveyed the cramped quarters, including Giles's messy desk and the map of Foxpath Lake on the wall behind him. She noticed that a straight pin with a tiny, black ball on the head was sticking in the approximate location of the gold mine. A small fan atop a file cabinet was swinging in a semicircle, having virtually no success against the heat which had built up in the room.

Giles, his rather massive stomach straining at his shirt and belt, smiled apologetically. To Hillary, he looked like a stereotypical southern law officer, and yet she forced herself not to prejudge.

"Have you questioned the man I told you about?" she asked. "Does he appear to be a suspect?"

Giles issued a derisive chuckle.

"Ms. Garrett . . . I'm sorry but . . ." He hesitated,

shaking his head as he retrieved a serious expression. "The man you apparently saw at the gold mine, well, ma'am, his name is Jeremy Ketch, and, oh, I know that folks up around here call him the 'Foxpath Fiend', and everybody has a wild ass—'scuse me—a strange story about him, but I've got to tell you, that poor fella just isn't a murder suspect. Now that's the fact of the matter."

"But how can you be certain? I'm told he has a history of mental instability. How can you be so positive in saying he isn't capable of assaulting a little girl? Maybe something triggered his violent behavior. How do you know that isn't true?"

Giles shrugged helplessly.

"Ma'am . . . well, I don't. I don't. But, you see, I did go up and talk with his momma and with Jeremy. I did question them, so don't go, uh, thinkin' I didn't follow up on your concern. But I'm tellin' you, ole Jeremy Ketch may be scrambled in the brain some, but he's not—in my opinion, at least—he's not a bonafide murder suspect. A nuisance to Foxpath Lake, maybe. But no killer. No, ma'am, I just don't think so."

Though it led nowhere, Hillary continued to pursue her line of inquiry with Giles, giving up only when he dismissed her by saying, "Listen, I 'preciate your interest in this case, and, believe me, it's horrible business, the death of the Rybeck girl, but everything's bein' done that can be done. And right now, as you can see, I don't even have a secretary—she's off sick—and I'm tryin' my best to coordinate this investigation with the Foxpath police and the sheriff's department, and, on top of everything else, I've got newspaper folks up to my elbows most days. So there you are. All I can say is, we're workin' on the case. Doin' the best we can."

Which, to Hillary, wasn't good enough.

Late morning, Hillary needed a boost for her spirits.
I think you're pretty cool.
And she knew just who could give her that boost.
Stay away from Molly.
No, Clay hadn't really meant those words; he had said them in anger.

At the Foxpath Medical Center gift shop she bought a copy of *Entertainment Weekly* as well as the latest issue of *Vanity Fair.* She hoped Molly Brannon would be impressed that she remembered the girl's interest in show business.

She also bought a bracelet of small wooden blocks spelling out the name "Molly." With her treasures in hand, she started to the children's ward, and found that along the way she wished Clay would be visiting his sister.

Despite the abrupt manner in which he had ended their talk a few days ago, Hillary couldn't keep her thoughts from occasionally turning to him, his unassuming good looks a draw. But more so, she was attracted to his sensitivity—*his love*—for Molly.

Clay Brannon's different from other guys.

And she liked that difference, while wondering how he had developed such a negative impression of her—such an inaccurate perception of her.

Give me some time. I can change that, she challenged herself. *I'm not a spoiled rich girl.*

At the nurse's island, she introduced herself and then said, "I'm here to see Molly Brannon."

By the puzzled expression on the receptionist's face, Hillary guessed that Molly's ruse had been discovered. She could almost hear Molly hugging her delight and saying, *I told 'em this big story 'bout how you were my cousin and I hadn't seen you for years . . .*

The young black woman glanced over her shoulder at an older woman who stepped forward and said, "I'm sorry, miss, but Molly Brannon . . ."

Hillary heard the remainder of the sentence, but the information did not register at first. Even when she felt the woman's hand on hers, even when she heard additional words, words of consolation, there was something too unfathomable to respond to.

And then she plunged with the sudden rush of sadness.

It was like being carried over a waterfall, not knowing where the building torrent of emotion would carry her.

Ten

The phone booth was stifling.

And it made its occupant feel small. Very small and very vulnerable.

But it was a place to hide.

The monstrous explosion had shaken everyone from sleep. One explosion of light. Then another.

Someone shouting, "Go back! Mop level 4!"

The panic made shadows appear. Horrible shadows with demonic shapes.

And then the burning. And eyes watering. And mucous filling the nose. A taste of copper pennies.

The occupant held on to the receiver.

". . . a bad man . . ."

It was difficult to breathe.

The aches and the fatigue.

There wasn't enough room. The thunderclap of sound echoed. The phone booth seemed to shake, threatened to topple over.

It was a little girl's voice.

Out there. And in the phone booth.

Something like a sonic boom flash was so bright that it turned midnight to noon. Yet, even at noon, the shadow of a child rose from beneath the surface of the lake. Calling.

* * *

Clay had seen Hillary at Molly's funeral, and though he had barely acknowledged her presence, he had appreciated her being there and her quiet offer of consolation. Hillary's pretty face was in his thoughts as he sat on the living room floor and sorted through Molly's things: tapes mostly, posters, a few books and magazines, her wigs, and one unopened box of Milk Duds.

He sighed heavily.

He had saved his tears for moments when no one else was around, and he knew that Molly would not want him to cry. She would not, in fact, want him to grieve.

Shine on, she would say.

When his mother suddenly entered the room, he glanced up as she moved toward the sofa and sat down cautiously, almost reverently, as if she were performing some delicate operation and must not be disturbed.

"You, okay?" he said.

She smoothed her dress and pressed her lips together tightly to stave off any tears. She nodded.

"It touched my heart," she said, "to see some of the parents of the other kids on Molly's floor at the funeral— like they's part of our family."

Clay couldn't resist the temptation for sarcasm.

"Yeah, closer to Molly than some members of her own family."

His mother stared at the floor.

"What do you want to do with all that?" she asked. "I'm thinkin' I'll give Molly's clothes to the Goodwill in town. What about them things?"

Clay lifted a Jimi Hendrix tape and smiled.

"I got to hold on to most of this. Too many good memories. Can't let go of them." Then he put down the tape and reached for the box of Milk Duds. "But this . . . I know where this is going. I'm gonna take this to Bradley, the chocolate stealer."

His mother looked puzzled.

"What on earth?"

"One of Molly's leukie friends," Clay explained. "A smartass kid, but I think he really liked Molly. Everybody on the floor did. It would have been impossible not to like Molly."

"She was my dear, sweet child." His mother patted her lips; her chin quivered, and the room filled with silence for a minute or more.

Then she cleared her throat and said, "Clay, you know . . . I wasn't able to get word to your father . . . about Molly . . . until it'd been too late for him to make it to the funeral, but I talked with him and, course, he was heartbroken to hear 'bout his only daughter, and he said he'd be comin' on home real soon to take care of us and—"

"Take care of us! Is that what he said? Take care of us? He's not capable of taking *care* of anybody. If he does come around here I'm gonna tell him to keep the hell away. What do we need him for? He doesn't give a damn about us. Not about me. Not about Molly. And I doubt, I really doubt, that he cares that much about you."

"That's not true," she snapped. "That is *not* true. He wants somethin' better for me and that's why he went away lookin' for it. You should've heard him on the phone when I had to tell him our Molly had passed . . . why, it tore the man up. So don't go tellin' me he don't care. He cares all right."

"About himself, maybe. About being gone. Which is what I'm fixing to be."

Clay got to his feet. The verbal standoff was just that. An exchange headed nowhere.

"Clay?"

Reluctantly, he stayed a moment longer.

"What?"

"Well, I know how much . . . how much you loved Molly and she loved you. I know you'll miss her, and I will, too. Just because I couldn't bring myself to be with her these last days doesn't mean I didn't love her. Don't ever think I didn't love her."

There was pleading in her tone.

Clay said nothing, but when he walked by her he reached out and squeezed her shoulder.

He was scheduled for the evening shift, and that gave him time to bike to where he could be alone. Knifing through the wind felt good; when he reached his destination it was as if he had been cleansed.

The late afternoon heat was boiling up the possibility of a shower. As Clay listened to distant thunder, he strolled from headstone to headstone. The Children's Graveyard ticked with the incessant heat.

Molly belongs here.

It was an odd thought, and yet it was true. To Clay, the anonymous, weed-choked cemetery given over to the re-mains of children seemed a far more appropriate final resting place for his sister than did the new and freshly mown section of the cemetery in town.

But what did it matter where she was buried?

Molly was alive in his thoughts and in his heart.

Molly. The Girl Who Sailed Away.

Molly . . . the one for whom he would do anything.

He was standing quite still when her words pressed in upon him.

I want you to promise me you'll use your imaging ability to help catch whoever killed that little girl.

A promise.

One he would have to keep.

No matter how dangerous it might become.

And the first step in fulfilling that promise would be to contact Hillary. And to apologize for treating her rudely.

With that thought, he left the small graveyard and began biking toward town, intent upon surprising the produce manager at Kroger's by clocking in early for work.

He would give Hillary a call tomorrow.

And then . . . well, he would see where the summer led.

Because his mouth has dry, he wheeled in at the Quik Shoppe for something cold to drink. The air conditioning inside the convenience store invited him to linger over the choice of bottled thirst quenchers in the cooler. He took his time selecting a Sprite, paid for it, and then stepped out into the oven-like air again.

And stared at the phone booth near the store.

And the man in it.

It appeared to be the Foxpath Fiend.

Clay felt his heart race.

He watched as the man twisted around in the booth as

if he were trapped and confused. The man was wearing a deer hunter's camouflage outfit from head to toe. Clay also noticed that he was carrying a small rifle, probably a toy.

For a few seconds longer, the man struggled with the fold-in door to the booth. Clay could hear him growl, a sound which gave him a slight chill. Then at last he succeeded in freeing himself. He burst from the booth and glanced immediately at Clay. And though the man said nothing, nor did he make any kind of threatening gesture, there was something in that look, something fierce in those dark eyes which made Clay involuntarily take one step back.

And then the Foxpath Fiend, for it definitely was he, rambled off into the woods.

Clay was drawn to the phone booth.

Walking his bike over to it, he began to feel queasy. He reasoned that his body could be reacting to the heat, and yet he knew better.

There's something here.

Ten feet or so from the booth he halted.

Something.

If he were to reach out and touch the booth and concentrate, he would possibly know. But the very thought of doing so cramped his every muscle. His head began to pound.

It was as if the Foxpath Fiend had left something there.

Something so dark and terrifying that Clay's body was warning his mind to stay away.

Something.

Eleven

"I'm afraid," said Hillary.

Charmian picked up the tray with the young woman's half-eaten sandwich on it and brushed at some crumbs on the deck furniture.

"It surely be not the first time your folks have a big fight. Now I know that's right. I've been hearin' more than one since I been workin' for 'em."

Hillary reached out for the woman's arm.

"Charmian, please put that down. Come and sit. I need someone to talk to. Please."

With studied reluctance, the woman sat down opposite Hillary and fixed her attention momentarily on the lake and the dwindling splendor of the sunset.

"This be my favorite time of the day," she said, nodding. "So peaceful and all. Like one of the psalms you read in church. If your folks be spendin' time gazin' at God's glory out there, maybe they'd feel the peace of it all."

Hillary smiled.

"You would think that would be true. But this last fight, I don't know. When Daddy stormed off, I sensed that some boundary had been crossed. Some point of no return. Mother can't seem to help herself, and both refuse to get counseling."

"Missus Garrett should oughtta be comin' home directly. This is her day for shoppin' in Montgomery with her friends."

"I'm surprised she still has any," Hillary followed. "Who wants a drunk for a friend? Oh . . . I know I shouldn't call her that, but that's what she is. My mother is a drunk."

"Honey, you listen now to Charmian . . . all this, this fightin' 'tween your folks. It's gist somethin' they got to do, and it hurts you, hurts you bad, I know. But you can't keep 'em from fightin' and you can't keep 'em goin' apart if that's what they gone do."

The surface of the lake, so serene, so inviting to the eye, drew Hillary into a collage of images from the past.

"I used to believe it was my fault," she said. "The fighting between them. I was so afraid they would get a divorce. I hated that word. I'm not sure why. I had several friends whose parents had divorced, so it wasn't that I was unfamiliar with it. It just seemed . . . unthinkable that it should happen to mine. I really thought I should be able to keep it from happening. I even imagined running away, thinking that when they discovered I was missing, they would be so worried they would come together and search for me, and when they found me they would be so happy they would never fight again."

Charmian smiled knowingly.

"Like somethin' from a fairy tale story."

"Yeah. A fairy tale. Far from reality."

Charmian was looking at her with deep sympathy.

"You be havin' a right bad week or so, what with your folks fightin' and you losin' your job and then havin' them funerals."

"Two funerals within a week," said Hillary. "I've never

had that happen. And they were such sad ones—the Rybeck girl and then, and then . . . Molly Brannon."

"She must been special, this Brannon girl?"

"Yes, very special. Not that Leigh Rybeck wasn't also. It's just that I never got to meet her—except perhaps on the phone. But Molly Brannon stole my heart in no time at all. And I like her brother, Clay, though he's kind of difficult to get to know."

Hillary could sense that Charmian was fidgeting. The woman did not like to sit when she was on duty. "I'm not no 'goldbricker,' " she would often explain. And so Hillary accelerated her thoughts, hoping to get a drop or two more of the woman's earthy, quiet wisdom.

"Charmian, have you ever gone through a period in your life when you feel like you're being swept along in a flooded stream? Like you have no control over events. And you don't know where you're headed. At the mercy of forces you can't understand. I feel like that."

With a hint of a smile, Charmian said, "Many's the time I have."

"How do you get through such times? I feel so unhappy and depressed and . . . and helpless."

"Hmm, well, honey . . . in the bad times I pray some. And I be patient. Till the good times come on back. They will."

"Patience," Hillary whispered, more to herself than to Charmian. "I don't believe I have any. I feel restless and miserable." She squeezed Charmian's wrist and added, "Hey, thanks for listening. I'm going for a walk to sift through some things."

Charmian raised a finger of caution.

"You be careful, honey. This lake, it's just not be safe bein' 'round here no more."

"I'll watch myself. Why don't you go on home. I'll wait up for Mom."

Charmian was right, of course.

As Hillary turned from her driveway onto the asphalt road and let the twilight surround her, she sensed that the safe haven Foxpath Lake had always seemed to be had changed.

The death of Leigh Rybeck had somehow altered the mood—even the landscape—of the place. Could the little girl's murderer be lurking among the sapling pines which lined the road? Donnie Ray Giles would have said, "No." His best theory was that a drifter, the seasonal kind who made their appearance at the lake every summer, had done the deed. And moved on. The killer's motivation? Difficult to say. It hadn't involved sexual assault. There was no robbery. Could it simply have been a case of Leigh Rybeck showing up at the wrong place at the wrong time?

I pretended a bad man . . .

The words had lost none of their capacity to terrify her.

Leigh Rybeck's words? Or some other little girl's? Innocent words? Or a dark prophecy which had come true?

Clay Brannon might know the answer. At the very least, and without any material evidence to support her view, she had come to believe that Clay's rumored powers were real. Perhaps she believed it because she wanted to—because she was attracted to Clay, to something about him she could not pin down—and, perhaps more so, because

Molly believed in those powers. Molly Brannon believed her brother could help track down a killer.

Up ahead, where the road swung toward a point, she saw John Jaggery in his front yard, moving a hose and an oscillating sprinkler unit. As usual, he was wearing a dark jumpsuit and a white golf cap. She smiled at the sight of him struggling with the hose as the twilight appeared to melt around him.

"Hey, Mr. Jaggery!" she called out as she approached.

He looked up, startled at first, but then when he recognized her he waved.

"Well, my dear, good evening."

She walked up his driveway, admiring the neatness of his yard. The groupings of azaleas and gardenias and the almost manicured effect of his Bermuda grass. And, closer to him, she chuckled to see that the sprinkler had wetted his glasses and jumpsuit.

"You're not out here playing in your sprinkler, are you?"

He grinned expansively.

"You caught me. You surely did. It's the best way to stay cool. Can you believe this heat? And dry . . . why, did you know we haven't had more than an inch of rain since late April?"

"I've noticed that the lake's going down," she said.

"That it is. That it is. Say, can you sit and keep me company for a spell?"

"Sure. I'd like that. I didn't mean to interrupt your watering, though."

He threw his hands in the direction of the hose and sprinkler.

"It's a losing battle. Mother Nature's going to have to

come through with some rain—watering doesn't get the job done. Let me go check on something inside, and then we'll sit out on the back porch. How's that sound?"

Moments later, Hillary was sitting among the jungle of plants on Jaggery's screened porch. There were potted plants everywhere and a philodendron plant which snaked up two walls and along the ceiling of the rectangular porch.

When she turned to say something to Jaggery about the menagerie of plants, she caught him looking over his shoulder into the house, a wash of concern on his face. But then he sensed that she was watching him and spun around.

"These are all Velma's," he said. "I just haven't been able to bring myself to get rid of them."

"The philodendron is remarkable. At the rate it's growing, you're going to have to lock the porch door or it'll come strangle you in the night."

"You're right. You're right. Like one of those sci-fi movies from the 50s."

"Or *Little Shop of Horrors*," she followed, and he nodded in agreement.

He had brought out a pitcher of iced tea and they sipped at tall glasses of it and relaxed.

"I hate to bring up anything negative," said Jaggery, "but my sources in town tell me your radio career has been put on hold. If so, then I'm very sorry."

"Your sources are correct, and, in a way of course, I'm sorry, too. But I suppose I understand what Mr. Smith was facing. I should be looking for another job. The restaurant at the marina needs a nightshift waitress, or I could do like some of my friends and be a sun bum. You know, lie out and work on my tan for half the day and spend the other half at the mall. Or on the phone."

"That doesn't sound like Hillary Garrett."

"I'm glad to hear you say that. Lately I've been accused of being spoiled and always getting my way."

"Whoever said that doesn't know you at all."

"No . . . unfortunately he doesn't. Anyway, as far as work is concerned, I haven't really been in the mood to work. Mom and Dad are fighting again and then . . . well, I went to two funerals. Leigh Rybeck and Molly Brannon."

"Sad business," Jaggery murmured. "Terribly sad. The Brannon girl, she was Clay's sister, isn't that right?"

"Yes, a darling little girl. I only really met her once, but she was totally charming. And she adored Clay."

Jaggery patted a finger thoughtfully at his temple.

"Clay Brannon. Hmm, you know, I could never quite figure him. Sensitive but distant. His sister's illness troubled him greatly, and his father apparently is a derelict. He and his mother have had it rough financially, or so I've heard. I've just never . . . never been able to warm to Clay."

Hillary was surprised to hear Jaggery's admission.

"I want him to help me," she said.

"Help you?"

It was Jaggery's turn to be surprised. Hillary could detect it in his tone.

"The murder of Leigh Rybeck and the possible connection with the phone call I received on 'Just Pretend' have forced me to want to get involved with finding the murderer."

"Shouldn't you let our law enforcement officials take care of that?"

She shook her head vigorously.

"I've dealt with them, particularly with Donnie Ray Giles, and I don't have much confidence in them."

"Donnie Ray Giles . . . well, I think I understand. A good ole boy, as they say, but Donnie's not exactly Sherlock Holmes. Just please be careful, my dear."

There was more she wanted to confide—her belief in Clay's wild talent and her encounter with the Foxpath Fiend—but the weariness in Jaggery's expression suggested that it was time to say good night. When she indicated that she should go, he said, "May I escort you home? I'd rest easier if you'd allow me to. There's a meanness in the air these days. Who can explain it?"

Though they exchanged only a bit of small talk, she was glad she didn't have to walk along the dark road alone. At her front door, Jaggery said, "My dear, just one small piece of advice: go slow in whatever relationship you're developing with Clay Brannon. He may be a fine young man . . . oh, I don't know what I'm saying except that I don't want to see you get hurt."

"Fair enough," she said. "You're still my counselor."

Hillary was ready for bed when the phone rang.

She had been thinking about Clay, wishing she had given him a call in addition to the sympathy card she had sent to him and his mother.

And she had been glancing at the clock, wondering why her own mother was not home yet—it was nearing ten o'clock. The phone jangled the mix of thoughts. She feared it was bad news.

"Hello?"

The hesitation, the uneven, heavy breathing knifed at her.

"Hello? Please . . . who is this?"

A little girl's voice.

"The bad man . . ."

Hillary forced herself to be calm, but it was the sensation of having a gun pointed at her forehead. She shut her eyes tightly and said, "Please, who's calling?"

"The bad man . . . the bad man I pretended killed someone."

Hillary couldn't breathe.

She couldn't think.

She gritted her teeth and felt her heart swing up and beat hard in her throat.

The voice again.

"Help me."

And for a terror-blinding moment, Hillary thought she had spoken the words. But, no. Then she found her own voice.

"I will. Please, tell me who you are. Tell me where you are, and I'll help you. I promise I will."

"The bad man I pretended killed someone."

And the frustration broke her and she shouted, "Who are you!"

"The bad man . . ."

"Please," she whispered.

"The bad man I pretended killed someone . . . and he's going to kill again."

When Hillary woke the next morning, she was convinced, at first, that the call had come as part of a nightmare, a lucid dream which had unfolded with frightening clarity.

But then, as she gradually shook free of her fitful sleep, she realized it had been no dream. When the caller had hung up, Hillary had immediately dialed the sheriff's department and then the office of Donnie Ray Giles to report the incident. In neither case was she taken as seriously as she felt she deserved, though the sheriff's department did suggest that a phone trace could be employed if she believed she would be called again.

The entire episode left her puzzled. And scared.

What did it mean?

The little girl's voice—she was almost totally certain it was the same as that of the caller to her show. So one theory had been laid to rest: that original caller had not been Leigh Rybeck. Then who? Obviously it was someone determined to stay in contact with Hillary—someone who had called her at home. Why? She ruled out a practical joke. And she could think of no one who harbored the kind of personal vendetta against her which might lead to such an unsettling call.

Nothing made sense.

And yet her fear was intensely real.

Downstairs, she had some orange juice and thought about calling someone. Perhaps John Jaggery. Perhaps the district attorney's office. Someone.

And that's when the kitchen phone rang.

Dear God.

She couldn't keep from trembling as she answered it.

"Hillary?"

"Yes?"

"It's Clay. Clay Brannon."

"Oh, Clay . . . thank goodness," she exclaimed. Her sigh of relief was long and deep.

"Is something wrong?"

"Well, it's just that . . . I'm just on edge this morning."

She could feel his hesitation. And then he said, "I'd like to talk to you this morning. Is that possible?"

"Yes. Yes, of course. But what about?"

"I . . . it's hard to explain over the phone. Could you meet me somewhere?"

"Yes, I suppose so. Where would you like to meet?"

"How about the Children's Graveyard . . . say in about thirty minutes?"

"Fine. I'll see you there."

"Thanks. Thanks, Hillary. I appreciate this."

Hillary wore the necklace and pendant Molly had given her. The small red heart and Band-Aid. And the echo of Molly's words.

The whole world has got a broken heart.

You're so right, Molly.

Dew sparkled like diamonds as Hillary made her way through the taller grass and patches of low thicket and into the first sprinkling of gravestones. She saw Clay's bike leaning against a sapling pine. And then, a few yards beyond, she saw Clay sitting on a gravestone, holding a Walkman, the earphones picking up glints of early morning sun.

When he heard her approach, he wheeled around and pulled off the earphones.

"Hi," he said, "you like Jimi Hendrix?"

She laughed nervously. "I don't even know who Jimi Hendrix is."

He looked disappointed.

"Only the greatest rock 'n roll guitarist of all time."

"Oh, I see. No, I really don't listen to rock 'n roll. I'm sort of partial to Clint Black and Trisha Yearwood these days."

"They're country singers, aren't they? Hmm, too bad. But thanks for coming. Hope you didn't get too wet tromping through the weeds."

Their eyes met.

To Hillary, Clay was even more handsome than she recalled.

"Aren't you going to give me the shiver and quiver and silver and gold line?"

She was delighted to see his flush of embarrassment.

He recovered and smiled.

"You mean the old Cinderella line? 'Shiver and quiver, little tree,/Silver and gold throw down over me.' "

"Cinderella?"

"Yeah, an early version of the tale. That's the wishing line and . . . you see, I used to tell Molly this was a good place to say it—lots of good vibrations."

"Here?"

"Sure. I mean, in a ghostly way."

They stared at each other for a nearly uncomfortable run of seconds before Hillary said, "I miss her."

Clay lowered his head and then looked off to one side.

"Believe me. So do I. I miss her so much I ache."

She stepped closer to him and she reached out and grasped his hand and squeezed it. It was a natural act. It felt right.

"I want to show you what she gave me," said Hillary, lifting the pendant so that he could see it.

There was an easy flow to their conversation. No false starts or rough moments until Clay said, "I owe you an apology."

"For what?"

And it seemed, ironically, that a space widened between them.

"For some things I said to you the last time we were here. Stupid remarks about you always getting your way. I apologize. I really do."

Warmth flooded her throat. The space between them dissolved.

"I try not to be a spoiled rich kid. I certainly don't want you to think of me as one."

"I haven't given you a chance," he followed, "to show who you really are. Molly liked you. She was always a great judge of character—me, I've got a bad habit of categorizing people. Forgive my dumb comments, okay?"

She nodded.

"If you'll pardon me for not knowing Jimi Hendrix."

"You got it."

She could tell that he wanted, needed, to say something more. And she wanted, almost desperately, to tell him about last night's call.

An awkward silence fell around them.

It was Clay who broke it. His words sounded rehearsed. A bit like something from a junior-high skit.

"I made a promise to Molly," he began. "Right before she died, I agreed to . . . help try to find whoever it was who murdered that little girl. I agreed to use this . . . this thing I can do sometimes. This ability to see things. To see people. To see the image of themselves they've left behind. I thought I should tell you."

"I'm glad you told me. Because there's something I want to share with you. I was at home last night, and I got a phone call, and . . ."

As the summer sun rose higher, she recounted the call, and they began to talk about it. And they fell willingly into each other's thoughts.

In that innocent landscape of the dead, a relationship was given birth, a friendship breathed, and the heart of something more than friendship began its first, tentative beats.

Twelve

Hillary couldn't sleep that night.

Her thoughts raced like some small machine locked in a mechanical fury and slightly out of control. A machine without design or function.

She had heard her mother come upstairs from watching television. Lately, the woman spent hours lost in movies, lost in them as if they were merely an alternative source of inebriation. Hillary steered clear of her for the most part, though she felt guilty for not pushing the woman to get help.

There's too much going on in my life.

That was Hillary's excuse. A pretty good one. But not one which allowed her to rest. And thus she found herself out on the deck as midnight approached, caged by her restlessness and wondering whether she would be able to sleep at all.

Macbeth hath murdered sleep.

She had to smile at the sudden and unexpected way in which some circuit of memory had lighted up that line from her English class. Shakespeare's plays had been tough going for her, and yet she had enjoyed *Macbeth,* one of world literature's great tragedies, but wasn't it, she reasoned, also a murder mystery? Who killed the king? And why? And what about those witches?

Hillary felt in the midst of a real murder mystery. Not a Shakespearean drama. But real events in east Alabama, her part of the world. Foxpath Lake. Her home. And echoes of a call from a little girl.

. . . and he's going to kill again.

If the police or the sheriff's department or Donnie Ray Giles could have heard that voice, they would have believed it, just as she believed it. Somewhere in this part of the world someone was planning to kill. Again.

But who was it? And how did that little girl know? Who was she? The questions seemed endless. Each question seemed to give birth to a new question until her thoughts tumbled like clothes in a dryer. Answers eluded her.

Below the deck, a single light on a pole at the end of the Garrett's dock called to her. Called her closer to the lake. Heeding its call, she walked down the steps and onto the walkway until she reached the edge of the dock and let the cool, dark shimmer of the lake hold her in its splendor.

She thought of Clay.

Brief, romantic thoughts. Snatches of scenes. And then chided herself, because such thoughts seemed so inappropriate in light of further horror which she believed was imminent.

I have to find that little girl.

And the killer has to be stopped.

To her left the dark surface of the lake smothered the reflection of the single light. The lake seemed to breathe like a heavy sleeper. It was beautiful. She heard a soft, purling sound, a liquid sound, and assumed it might be some night creature—a muskrat perhaps—out in search of food.

When she saw the man in the boat she nearly screamed.

Though his identity was completely hidden, she knew. The certainty rushed through her like a gust of wind.

The Foxpath Fiend.

There. Alone in a boat. Moving toward the dock.

He knows I suspect him.

As she turned to run, she noticed that the boat was moving faster, that it was headed at an angle which would cut her off if she didn't sprint for the house. But she found that her legs wouldn't respond as she needed them to. She stifled a cry and her lungs suddenly filled with so much air that she thought they would burst.

"Hillary? Hillary, is that you?"

The voice came from out on the lake. A familiar voice.

She stopped struggling to run and turned as a skiff slipped into view.

"Clay? Oh my God, I'm glad it's you."

He chuckled nervously as he poled up against a dock post.

"Here, catch this tie-down rope," he said. "Guess you couldn't sleep either, huh?"

When he was on the dock, standing with her, she realized that she was trembling. He touched her shoulder reassuringly.

"Geez, were you expecting the Creature From the Black Lagoon?"

"Worse," she replied. "I thought you were the Foxpath Fiend."

"He's the killer," said Clay.

They had walked hand in hand up to the deck where

she invited him to sit down, and she was surprised at how pleased she was to have him there.

Growing impatient when she did not respond, he said, "You don't think I'm serious, do you?"

"No. No, Clay, it's not that. In fact . . . well, he seems the most obvious suspect, but it also seems that no one else on Foxpath Lake views him that way. They think he's borderline nutso but not a murderer—not even *capable* of murdering."

"Anybody's capable of murdering. *Anybody*. And here's something else: the little girl who called you . . . I've got a theory about her. I think she saw the Foxpath Fiend. I think she saw Jeremy Ketch, and the impact of seeing him was so strong that she can't get the image of him out of her mind."

"But just because she may have *seen* him doesn't mean he's the killer."

"I know. I know. But listen to this: the other day I saw Ketch, and guess where he was?"

"At the gold mine again?"

"No. At the Quik Shoppe. In the phone booth there. And he wasn't wearing that same outfit he usually wears. This time he had on deer hunter's camouflage. I watched him, and when he left I went over to the phone booth and I . . . I got this feeling—"

Suddenly Hillary couldn't contain her excitement.

"Did you *see* something?"

"Not exactly. It's just a hunch . . . that's all I can say. That phone booth—I believe it was the one, you know, that the little girl who called you the first time—it was from that booth, and the 'bad man'—I believe it's Ketch, the Foxpath Fiend."

Hillary studied Clay's face. His long, black hair caught the deck lighting and absorbed it. And his peace symbol earring made her think, momentarily, of Molly.

"If you went back to that phone booth . . . oh, I don't know, there's still something about this . . ."

Clay looked at her. A hard, disappointed look.

"You doubt it, don't you? You doubt what I can do."

She shook her head.

"No. No, I didn't say that."

"You didn't have to. Okay . . . time for a demonstration."

"Clay, no. No, you don't have to prove anything to me."

"I think I do."

He glanced around, then centered on the table and the chairs where they were sitting.

"Please, Clay . . . it isn't necessary."

He sighed.

"I can tell you the last person who sat in this chair."

His voice was tremulous and filled with an uncertain bravado.

And she could tell that there was no point in further protest—he was determined to do what he felt he must do. In a self-conscious gesture, she pushed her chair back from the table as if to give him room.

It was mesmerizing to watch the process. To watch him grow silent and to sense that he was asking his body to cooperate fully. Muscles. Nerves. Every vein and artery. Every breath from his lungs and every beat of his heart. He closed his eyes. He reached out to the round, glass-topped table and rested his fingers there as a pianist would on a keyboard.

Seconds passed.

She could see a sheen of sweat on his upper lip and forehead, his jaw tighten, and the muscles of his forearm ripple. He was gritting his teeth. His pained expression was similar to grimaces she had witnessed on the faces of weightlifters; only in this case, Clay was not interacting with a barbell but rather with another dimension.

In less than a minute, he rocked back on his chair and shook his head as if to shake off a shock of some kind. His eyelids fluttered and the rest of his body appeared to go limp. When he opened his eyes, he looked as if he did not feel well.

"May I have some water, please?" he said.

Hillary dashed to the kitchen, and when she handed him the glass she was relieved to see that he had a cautious, perhaps even a slightly confident, smile on his lips.

"A black woman in a yellow dress. An elderly woman—not real, real old, though. And . . . she didn't want to be sitting here for some reason. I don't know . . . I couldn't see anything more."

He looked at Hillary, a hopeful look.

She nodded.

"Charmian. Our maid. Yes, she probably was the last person to sit in that chair, and you're quite right—she doesn't like to sit down on the job."

"Okay, good. I still have it . . . I don't want it, but I still have it."

"How do you feel?"

"Wiped out. That's how I always feel."

"It's incredible."

"It's more like . . . a burden of some kind. I hate it. And it scares me."

"Why? I mean, if you used it to perform something

very useful—like catching a murderer—wouldn't that make you feel great? I think that's how it would make me feel."

He shook his head and looked away.

"No. You don't understand. It's one thing picking up the image of your maid, you know. A . . . a good image, you know, no bad vibrations, but making contact with the image of a killer, I . . . I don't know what that would do . . . physically, mentally. It might be like a tremendous jolt of electricity."

"Clay, I don't want you to try anything that could harm you. I care about you. I mean, I do want to stop the murderer. With all my heart, I do. But not if it means risking you getting hurt."

When he looked into her eyes again, she saw something much softer there. Obviously it had pleased him to hear that she cared about him—*and I do*—and he appeared to be searching for precisely the right response.

"I've really been wrong about you," he said.

She smiled and cocked her head to one side.

"How so?"

"You're serious about this. About what's happened. The murder and stopping the murderer. You're serious about being involved with it. To be honest, I always thought that you were the kind of person who took up causes without really believing in them. Someone who did it because it looked good to others, you know, to teachers and other adults . . . but I've misjudged you. You're not like that."

"Not a rich bitch?"

They both laughed softly.

And in the moment grew closer.

"What impression have you always had of me?" he probed.

"Hmm, that's kind of an egotistical question, isn't it?"

He smiled.

"Yeah. You got me. Sorry."

"No. I'll answer it. I've always seen you as smart and sensitive and creative, but I wonder . . ."

"Wonder what?"

Her hesitation threw both of them off balance.

"Perhaps I shouldn't say this," she began. "But I wonder why Mr. Jaggery doesn't seem to have a higher opinion of you. He as much as warned me against developing a relationship with you."

"Jaggery. Yeah, well, maybe he's just offering some good neighborly advice about all young men. I don't know. Truth is, yeah, he and I have never hit it off. You like him, don't you?"

"Very much. I mean, I respect him. He's a good man. And he really is a good neighbor. He's been helpful to me—the nightmare of all this. He's been concerned about me. I've needed that."

"A nightmare, yeah. For me lately, too. Molly. And . . . did I tell you Molly's dream? She had a dream about me and you."

"No. I'd love to hear it."

"She said she dreamed that you and I climbed down into a big, dark box of some kind because we were trying to save someone. We had heard someone crying—down in the box, I guess—you know, a kid or a child. She didn't say whether we ended up saving him."

"Or her. You said 'him,' but I think Molly would have dreamed it was a little girl we were saving."

"Yeah, you're probably right. Anyway, that's her dream."

"Prophetic, maybe?"

"You got me. I can see images of where people have been, but whether dreams show the future—that's out of my league."

They said nothing more for a few seconds. Clay shifted in his chair. Hillary could tell that he felt he should go. She didn't want him to.

"What's next?" she asked.

"What's next is, I better get my butt home. I'm glad, you know, I'm glad I got to see you."

"I am, too—glad I got to see *you*."

"Hillary, I'm gonna shadow Ketch. Again, it's just a hunch. I could be way off. I think he may be the killer. I'm gonna trail him, especially now that you've had another call."

"That call," she said, "it haunts me. I'm going to do whatever I can to find out who it is. I assume it's someone on the lake—maybe I'll just go house to house. It seems like I'm overlooking something so obvious but—"

"Hey," he said, "sleep on it." He smiled, and she felt that he embraced her with his eyes. "Walk me down to the skiff," he added.

Before stepping into the skiff, he turned to her and put his hands on her shoulders.

"Take care, okay?"

"I will."

And then he leaned down and kissed her on the lips, surprising her, pleasing her.

"I should have listened to Molly," he said. "She told

me you were cool. She had a way of knowing. Wise beyond her years."

Hillary agreed.

"Good night, Clay," she said. "Will you call me if you turn up something on our Fiend?"

"I'll do it. Hey, you know . . . I think we'll make a pretty good team."

Thirteen

Donnie Ray Giles ate a big breakfast whenever he was worried about something. Accordingly, the plate before him was heaped with scrambled eggs, grits, sausage patties as well as sausage links, and four biscuits—freshly buttered and jellied—strawberry jelly. Lots of it. And a large cup of coffee in a very substantial ceramic cup. Giles hated plastic cups and plastic forks and knives.

At 6:00 A.M., he was among the early, early crowd at the Foxpath Lake Marina Grill. The sprinkling of others included a few old men—retirees—and two or three fishermen, the latter not quite awake yet. Giles sat at the counter, and to his left he received a panoramic view of the lake, which this morning had a thin veil of mist hovering over it.

A scene which always made him feel a touch uneasy.

"How are your eggs, Officer Giles?"

The sweet voice issued from a bright-eyed, blond young woman whose name was Debra Peaches—really and truly her name—though everyone who came into the Grill on a regular basis called her "Peachface." Giles liked her. In fact, the first summer she worked at the Grill he thought he might have been in love with her. He enjoyed having her refer to him as "Officer Giles." No one else gave him that kind of innocent respect.

But Peachface was innocent. Just like Drew.

"Fine 'n dandy, sweetheart. If they was any better, you'd have to mount 'em on your wall like a trophy buck. Say, what's goin' on at 'Foxtails' these days?"

The young woman positioned her left leg, stiffened by multiple sclerosis, against the counter and said, "Swimming. Everybody's swimming. I saw your brother Drew there yesterday, and he showed me his baseball card collection. He has lots of cards of Bo Jackson."

"Oh, I know that for sure. I do."

Giles fought a moment with the image of his much younger brother, severely crippled by MS, maneuvering his virtually useless arms to handle his beloved cards. Drew was a permanent fixture at the camp for the handicapped—or "handy capable," the culturally correct description.

"Everybody's kinda scared, too," she followed. "Because, you know . . . of what happened to Leigh Rybeck. But the counselors tell everyone, 'Don't be afraid. The police won't let anything bad happen,' and I'm not scared because I know Officer Giles—you." She hesitated to giggle. "And I know you won't let anything bad happen. So, I'm just working and not being very scared."

At the other end of the counter someone called out for more coffee and the young woman limped away. Giles's throat burned. Not from the coffee. But from . . . well, it would have been difficult, extremely difficult, for him to pin down why he was feeling so unsettled.

The murder of Leigh Rybeck was a good place to start. Followed closely by Hillary Garrett's persistence in bugging him about the investigation. And her allusion to two curious phone calls she had received, and, most of all, to her suspicions about Jeremy Ketch.

Giles tried a forkful of scrambled egg and it rested there on his tongue like some strange formation of crystals. He had trouble washing the eggs down with a gulp of coffee. He was hungry—famished—and yet food was proving a real effort to swallow.

He kept imagining a string of shadows.

With names.

His brother Drew and Ketch and Ketch's mother.

And Ketch's sister. If, indeed, it was his sister.

And John Jaggery.

And Samuel Wu-Wei, the old Chinaman.

And more shadows. Ghosts from the past.

The thing about Foxpath Lake was that, for Giles, it was like an extended family. Connections. Obligations. Memories. And he couldn't extract himself from them. Couldn't be his own man. For example, he owed his present job to the fact that John Jaggery, who probably had little respect for him, had gone to bat for him. Oh, he knew why.

Connections. Obligations.

And memories.

Of years ago, when he and Drew were living with foster parents, and the only other kids around to play with were Jeremy Ketch and a tiny girl named Patricia who Ketch thought of as his sister but who probably wasn't. Summers would find the foursome roaming the shore, pretending to be pirates up at the old gold mine or pretending to rob Sammy Wu-Wei who scratched out a living repairing and painting boats.

Summers were glorious idylls of the imagination.

Except for the final summer the four spent together.

They had two boats. One belonged to Ketch; his mother had bought it for him when he returned home from one of his numerous stays at an institution. The other boat, a skiff, belonged to Wu-Wei from whom they would occasionally "borrow" it.

Ketch would sail alone. He insisted upon it.

So that would leave Giles and Drew to team up, usually leaving a whining, crying Patricia on shore. Until one hot summer day, mid-morning as Giles recalled, Patricia's tantrum wore him down. He and Drew, who was quite young at the time, made room for her, and they rowed out perhaps a hundred yards. Into the deeper water.

Patricia—Ketch called her "Priddy Ann" because he couldn't say "Patricia"—could not settle herself at one end of the boat or the other.

She wasn't being careful.

Giles had told her to sit down. He had shouted at her. He had . . .

Reconstructing the scene for authorities later had not been easy. Drew was incapable of articulating what he had witnessed. Ketch had witnessed events from twenty or thirty yards away.

Giles had repeated one line over and over again.

"She wasn't being careful."

A body, strangely enough, was never recovered.

Sammy Wu-Wei shut down his business at the end of that summer.

Foxpath Lake held secrets.

But years had passed without tragic incident. But not, for Giles at least, without moments in which the almost palpable shadow of years gone by appeared before him. Often enough rising from the lake itself.

The shadow of a girl.

Giles knew what he had to do. Knew that Hillary Garrett had forced him to do it. He would have to stick close to Jeremy Ketch and not because he thought Ketch was a murder suspect. Hardly. There were other reasons. Good reasons.

"That newspaper woman's been looking for you."

Giles shook himself from his dark reverie.

"What's that, Peachface?"

She had her elbows propped on the counter and was twisting an unruly strand of hair.

"That woman. Ms. Boyle. From the Columbus, Georgia paper. Katie Boyle. She has red hair. I wish I had red hair. She wants to talk to you."

"About what, sweetheart?"

The young woman scrunched up her face and shaped her hands into claws and then whispered melodramatically, "The murder."

Giles knew he ought to smile at her histrionics.

But he couldn't.

Fourteen

Hillary warned herself not to get caught up in the swirl of things, in the dizzying, moment-to-moment pace of change with which this summer before her senior year had confronted her. And it had all started with a simple phone call.

I pretended a bad man.

Which had ignited a dark fire of rapid change: she had lost her job; had become engulfed in a murder mystery; had met a charming little girl and mourned her passing; and had developed a relationship with a young man . . . who saw images of people, images they had left behind like some unwanted part of themselves. Like a supernatural skin sloughed off.

He was a special young man.

Clay.

I think I'm falling in love with you.

And the thought gave her a pleasurable burn.

Seeing Clay the night before now seemed dreamlike. Romantic. Together they would pursue a murderer. It seemed impossible to believe—more like something you would read in a novel than like real life.

Clay thinks it's the Foxpath Fiend.

Maybe he's right.

Up and dressed, she clambered downstairs and found a surprise at the kitchen table: her mother.

"Juice and toast?"

Her mother was smiling, a cup of coffee cradled in her hands. She wasn't smoking. Hillary was pleased to see that.

"Where's Charmian?"

"I gave her the day off. Don't you have time for breakfast? You look tired, dear. Were you out late last night?"

Her mother's voice was throaty, the aftermath of so many years of smoking, and there were shadowy circles under her eyes, and yet she appeared to be making a concerted effort to be tuned in to the day.

"Talking with a friend," said Hillary. Then she glanced at her watch. "Oh, I didn't realize it was so late. I'll have some juice. Have you already had some?"

"Yes, dear. And two pieces of toast. And, now, my second cup of coffee. And I've been thinking about some things I wanted to say to you."

"Say to me?"

Hillary felt a sudden sensation that the floor was sinking beneath her.

"I never told you I was sorry about your radio job. I can talk to George Smith about getting it back if you like. Or your father could if Texas—or wherever he is this week—lets go of him. And what's this about your program being somehow connected with the murder of the Rybeck girl?"

Somewhat reluctantly, Hillary recounted most of the story, downplaying the amount of anxiety events had created within her.

"Enough about me," she concluded. "I'm concerned

about you, about how you're feeling and . . . about you and Daddy."

Frances Garrett reached out to tap lovingly at her daughter's hand. Her smile was warm and expansive and her eyes twinkled through a dull sheen; it was an attractive face, and in it Hillary could see what must have been, once upon a time, physically stimulating to her father.

"Your father and I . . . we have to fight our way through things to see where we are. To see whether we still care enough to keep fighting. I'm sorry you have to hear it. But when you hear only silence, then you'll know we've stopped trying. This other business—my 'little problem,' as one of my friends calls it—I'm sorry you've had to deal with that, too. Don't tell me I need help—of course, I do. But you see, dear . . . I have to convince myself that I can't do it on my own. I have to. Can you understand that?"

"I want to," said Hillary. "I want you to be on top of things, and for you and Daddy to work things out, if that's possible."

"Oh, wait," said her mother suddenly, "you got a call about thirty minutes ago. Someone from a newspaper. Here's the number. She asked to have you return her call."

There was more that Hillary wished to say to her mother. But most of it was unsayable. Held in subjection by doubt. Her mother was "talking" a pretty good game, and yet Hillary had heard it all before. It was now a matter of watching helplessly for the woman to hit bottom. And for a marriage to limp out its days.

The newspaper woman introduced herself as Katie Boyle and pressed to meet with Hillary at the Marina Grill in thirty minutes regarding "Just Pretend." Hillary agreed to the meeting but cautioned Boyle that the show had been canceled and that George Smith might be the person she should talk with. Boyle insisted upon seeing Hillary.

Exchanging good-byes with her mother, Hillary stepped out into the mid-morning heat and thought about Clay. She thought about how determined he had sounded in talking about trailing the Foxpath Fiend.

Please be careful.

She thought about Clay's good night kiss. And wanted more.

On the way to the Marina Grill, she passed the Quik Shoppe and noticed that someone was in the phone booth. She braked, made a U-turn, and pulled into the parking lot, surprised at how rapidly her heart was beating.

But that surprise was small compared with the one she experienced when she was close enough to identify the person in the booth.

Katie Boyle had magnificent red hair and was much younger than Hillary expected. And also more informed. The two of them sat in a booth where Boyle had been waiting over a cup of coffee. Hillary wanted nothing. Her stomach was already roiling from the shock and puzzlement of what she had witnessed at the Quik Shoppe.

He's not a suspect. I can't think that.

After a brief round of introductory small talk, Boyle asked, "Do you think the Foxpath Fiend murdered Leigh Rybeck?"

Momentarily speechless, Hillary gathered herself and tried, not quite successfully, to show that the question had not thrown her off balance completely.

"I . . . I thought we were going to talk about my radio show."

"From what I understand, the two are related. The call you received at the conclusion of your last show—was it merely a coincidence that the Rybeck girl was found murdered a few days later?"

"You'll have to ask the police or Donnie Ray Giles."

"I've talked with Giles. And a few other sources. It appears to me—call it a newspaper woman's intuition—that you're somehow near the center of everything. What makes you think the 'notorious' Foxpath Fiend is a good suspect? No one else around here does."

"Because I saw . . ."

Hesitating, Hillary glanced about the restaurant. She didn't like Boyle's aggressive style, and she was beginning to feel cornered.

"Look, I really don't care to discuss this. I've told the authorities what I know, and I think I should leave it at that. If you want to talk about my radio show, I will. But not the murder or any murder suspect."

She could see Boyle's jaw tighten and then the flicker of a smile.

"That's fine. I'll play it your way. Just one final question: what is Clay Brannon's involvement in this matter?"

Hillary's cheeks began to flush almost instantly. They warmed like a heating element on an electric range, and there was no possibility of disguising her reaction. Boyle had touched the right spot and knew it.

"I told you," she sputtered. "I told you I would only talk about my show. Now please—"

"What about this ability he has—a kind of psychic ability? Is he going to use it to identify the murderer?"

"No, I don't want to . . ."

Hillary was pushing away from the booth, but it seemed to her that she was moving in slow motion. Words and light and heat and color merged to form a surrealistic backdrop. She made it to the door with Boyle calling out after her. Distracted and confused, she drove away from the Marina Grill, wanting desperately to see Clay. To tell him about Katie Boyle and what she knew.

But also to tell him about the phone booth at the Quik Shoppe.

She drove along the road as it meandered around Foxpath Lake. It was impossible to think clearly. She kept hearing Boyle's questions, and she kept seeing . . . a man step from the phone booth. And, yes, she was positive she knew who it was.

Dave Tanner.

But so what?

No law against using a phone booth.

An innocent situation.

And probably a simple explanation as to why he was there making a call.

Or why there was a little girl with him.

"So are you gonna arrest me for trespassing?"

Clay stood on the sandy spill of shore annoyed by the manner in which Donnie Ray Giles had accosted him.

"No, sir, I'm not. This isn't private property, and you know that. But you also know that up that rise is the old gold mine and that area has been ribboned off for a criminal investigation. We don't need sightseers and curiosity seekers up there."

It was late afternoon, hot, with thunderheads gathering in the west. Clay had a couple of hours before he had to go to work; he had spent the afternoon looking for Jeremy Ketch. Without success.

He had put in his skiff, thinking that he would sneak up to the murder site and see what images lingered behind. But in attempting to mount the courage to do so, he had waited too long. On patrol, Giles had spotted him and had motored in to check out the scene.

He just wants to hassle me.

"It doesn't sound like the investigation has made much progress," said Clay.

Giles visibly bristled.

"And how many murder cases you solved, friend? We don't need amateur detectives gettin' in our way."

"I'd think you'd at least have some clues. Fingerprints. Footprints. *Suspects.*"

Hands on his hips, Giles chuckled to himself. Sweat rings spread out from his armpits. His face was also sweaty.

"Plastic gloves don't leave fingerprints," he said. "That girl was strangled by somebody wearin' plastic gloves. And by somebody who knew how to cover his tracks. Somebody—probably long gone from here—got his kicks from killin' and headed on down the road."

"I think you're wrong."

Giles glared at him. He lifted his wide-brimmed hat and swiped at the sweat on his forehead.

"You do, do ya? Well, seems that's what I've been hearin.' You and that Garrett girl apparently have your own theories—apparently you're pointin' a finger at Jeremy Ketch."

"We think he's a suspect, yeah."

"Well, let me tell ya somethin', Mr. Brannon." He squinted at Clay as if to add a layer of seriousness to his remarks. "It ain't Ketch. You're barkin' up the wrong tree on that one."

"Then who is it? There's evidence that the killer's still around. Evidence he's gonna kill again."

"You just go on about your bidness and let the proper authorities take care of investigating."

"The authorities appear to be needing help."

"We don't need no help. And here's a friendly piece of advice: stay the hell outta the way or you—and your girlfriend—could get yourselves in some mighty big trouble. Y'hear me?"

Clay stared at him.

"I hear you," he said.

Clay had repressed the terror.

For years, it seemed, he had wondered why the very sight of Jeremy Ketch, the Foxpath Fiend, sent waves of anxiety through him. Lingering on the shoreline that afternoon, he suddenly recalled the series of incidents which formed the foundation of his continuing fear. He had been six or seven at the time, and his mother had identified a shallow area of the lake along a spit of land covered by pines. He was allowed to swim there, though mostly he waded, searching the mossy bottom for anything interesting—crayfish, colorful rocks, or beer cans.

He wouldn't let me come out of the water.

At first, Ketch would happen by innocently enough; once or twice they had even skipped rocks together. But one day Ketch had stood on the shore, his hands raised menacingly, and had shouted out at young Clay, "You can't come out!"

And each time Clay had tried to escape from the water, Ketch had blocked him off.

"You damn little shit . . . stay out there till you drown yourself. And don't you go cryin' for help or it'll be the last time you cry for help."

Clay would plead.

And shiver and cry. And once he had gritted his teeth and advanced boldly to the shore only to be caught by Ketch.

"See what's gone happen," Ketch had exclaimed.

Clay had felt hands around his throat.

He had screamed.

Release left him shaken and chilled, his teeth chattering as he sprinted home with Ketch's words snapping at his heels: "Don't you go tellin' your momma or you'll get worse!"

So he never told his mother. Or anyone else.

And he never swam in the lake again without having one eye glued to the shore for signs of the approach of Ketch.

The horrible memory had faded . . .

But as Clay stood on the blisteringly hot shore, he found that his teeth were chattering.

"No wonder you feel the way you do about him," said Hillary.

"Yeah, but it's strange how I'd just sorta forgotten about

how Ketch used to terrorize me. Apparently, I repressed it. Until this afternoon . . . when it all came back."

"But, Clay, does it necessarily add up to murder? I mean, we agree that this man is a borderline psychotic or sociopath or whatever clinical term is appropriate . . . but a killer?"

They were on the Garretts' deck, Clay having poled over from his encounter with Donnie Ray Giles. Charmian had made them a pitcher of her famous lemonade.

"Do you have a better suspect?"

Hillary looked away.

"Maybe."

Then she told him about seeing Dave Tanner at the Quik Shoppe.

"I know it's a real flimsy reason for suspecting him," she said. "A coincidence. There have been so many co-incidences . . . and yet seeing him there with that little girl . . ."

"Could have been his sister," said Clay.

"Of course. And it would be simple enough to call the station and find out whether he even has a sister. I'm almost afraid to."

"Why?"

"I don't know. Dave's a good guy. He helped me a lot with my show. He was encouraging. That sort of thing."

"He ask you out?"

Hillary looked at Clay.

She smiled shyly because she thought she heard and saw a touch of jealousy in Clay's question and in his eyes.

"No . . . but I think he will. Unless he's—wow, this is weird."

"Would you go out with him? If he called five minutes from now, would you go out with him?"

"No."

"Why not?"

"Because—"

"Because he might be the killer? You can solve that. Ask him if he has a little sister. If he says 'no,' then tell him you don't date serial killers."

They both laughed, and Hillary swatted playfully at him. It was no laughing matter, they both acknowledged that. But laughing felt good in a summer in which laughter otherwise seemed unwelcome.

"No, I mean, I wouldn't go out with him because . . . I'm interested in someone else."

She was secretly delighted to see Clay blush.

"Oh, I see. That means I have competition, right?"

She touched his hand and leaned over and kissed his cheek.

"No," she said. "You don't."

"Good. The best news I've heard all day." He gazed at her, pulling her deeper into the loving side of himself. "Wish I didn't have to go to work tonight. I'd like to spend the evening with you. I might even have enough cash to spring for the shrimp special at the Marina Grill."

"Oh, hey," she exclaimed, "that reminds me. I haven't told you about Ms. Katie Boyle, have I?"

"No, you haven't."

"I need to, because I have a hunch she'll want to talk with you."

When Hillary had recounted her meeting with Boyle, Clay said, "She must have pretty good sources. She seems to know a lot. Who's she been talking to?"

"Good question."

"Well, I just hope she doesn't get in the way."

"What do you mean?"

Clay hesitated.

"Hillary, I don't think our valiant law enforcement officials are going to solve the murder case. I'm not even convinced they want to, or, at least, that they're trying very hard."

"I don't understand."

"I don't either. Except for this: for some reason Donnie Ray Giles doesn't want me trailing Ketch. It makes me suspicious. That's all."

"We both need to be careful," said Hillary. "I didn't handle the interview with Boyle very well. She smells a story, and my guess is that she senses you're a big part of that story."

Clay shrugged.

"I think Ketch is the story," he said. "What about you?"

She shook her head as if doing so would give her a new point of clarity.

"When I think about things as they are, I just keep hearing what that little girl said to me: 'The bad man I pretended killed someone . . . and he's going to kill again.' I can't get those words out of my head, and I just know that the horror hasn't ended yet."

"I agree."

Hand in hand, they walked down to where the skiff was tied.

"I'll think about you this evening," she said, giving him a hug.

"Hey," he said, "do you think Molly would forgive me for liking somebody who doesn't know Jimi Hendrix?"

"I hope so."

"I miss her, Hillary. God, how I miss Molly."

Hillary felt emotion clutch at her throat.

"Me, too," she whispered.

Fifteen

It was a moonless night.

A late evening shower had failed to cool the air more than a fraction. The water of Foxpath Lake was warm—almost too warm. Farther from the shore a thick mist was forming.

Clay floated on his back and thought of Molly.

He wished he could see stars—Molly loved to look at stars—but it was partly overcast and none were brightly visible.

He backstroked and thought of Hillary.

Can you believe this? Falling for a rich girl?

But he was.

All during his evening workshift at Kroger's he had fantasized about seeing her, about holding her in his arms and telling her that they should forget about the dark madness the summer had brought.

And belong to each other for the moment.

Yet, when he punched out at the end of his shift his thoughts turned to Jeremy Ketch. And some persistent, intuitive voice told him that the Foxpath Fiend might he on the prowl. So he had biked to the lake and he had poled his dad's skiff along the shore watching for any sign of Ketch. An hour of patrolling had nearly bored him to stone. He was tired and irritated with himself and decided that a swim would lift his spirits. Stripped down to his underwear, he had surrendered to the moist embrace of the lake as the mist gathered beyond him.

He dived below the surface into the dark nothingness, feeling the water lose its warmth the deeper he went. When he broke up through the ceiling again, he shook free of the clinging drops.

And that's when he noticed the point of light.

Because he was thirty or forty yards from the shore, he could not quite make out the source of the light, though he could detect that someone was carrying it. The shadowy block of a man, he guessed.

As silently as possible, he began moving forward, keeping focused as much as he could on the figure and the light as they covered the shoreline from his left to his right. Closer. The temperature seemed to be dropping. The mist thickening.

The light was a fisherman's lantern.

It was bobbing with the stride of the man. Yes, a man, a short man who was carrying something . . . something over his shoulder.

Two realizations struck Clay at once.

About twenty yards from the man, he stopped and treaded water. He recognized the man and feared that he knew what the man was carrying.

My God.

And then one more realization: the man had spotted him.

Clay held his nose and submerged.

He suspended himself in the watery darkness. He had to fight back panic and gain control of his fear. He had to decide what to do because the moment called for action:

the figure striding along the shore was almost certainly Jeremy Ketch, the Foxpath Fiend, holding a lantern in his right hand and carrying a body over his left shoulder.

A small body.

The body of a child.

Clay bubbled to the surface and saw that Ketch had moved a distance to his right, but the man must have heard the young man's stirring of the water, for he turned. And Clay experienced the old terror—*don't go tellin' your momma or you'll get worse.*

Nimbused by the lantern light, Ketch's face was a Halloween mask of horror. He stared straight at Clay, and the young man shuddered. A few tension-charged seconds passed, and then Ketch marched on.

Cautiously, keeping a distance of thirty yards or more, Clay followed, wading to the shore and throwing on his jeans. A light rain began to fall. Clay's teeth chattered, and up ahead the point of light bobbed eerily.

My God, he's killed again.

The rain intensified, and there was thunder and a flash or two of lightning. Ketch's form lumbered along the shore, quickening its pace.

Clay knew that he should stop, turn around and go for the authorities. For Giles or someone. That would be the right thing. The smart thing to do. But something too much like curiosity and fascination drove him on.

Where's he taking the body?

Clay tried but failed to get into the mind of a murderer. And he was at least mildly surprised to see Ketch come upon a small boat tied to a tangle of roots where the woods spilled out onto the shoreline.

Dropping the body into the boat, Ketch turned as if to

see whether he had been followed. Clay ducked out of sight, and then the man climbed into the boat, grasped the oars, and began to row out into the mist and rain.

He's going to dump the body in the lake.

Clay ran to the shore's edge and watched, spellbound, as the boat disappeared behind a curtain of mist. Feeling a shiver dance down his spine, Clay stood, mesmerized. The rain began to diminish. He stood yet for a minute longer until a final sensation would not release its hold.

Someone was watching him.

"You should have told Giles."

"I know. I know. But after I lost sight of Ketch, my main concern was to dodge whoever had tailed me."

"You're certain someone followed you?"

"Absolutely."

Clay reached out for Hillary's hand and added, "It'll be quicker if we go by skiff. I'll show you where I saw him."

Her balance not quite steady, Hillary stepped into the skiff, then sat down and folded her arms against her breasts.

"A cold morning for summer," she said, shivering slightly. "I couldn't imagine who was calling so early. I was afraid it was that little girl."

With the pole in hand, Clay pushed away from the dock and then looked down at Hillary.

"I'm sorry. I know it's not even 6:00 A.M. yet. But I wanted you to be with me. I needed you to be with me."

Hillary smiled, warmed by his words.

"I'm glad you did."

He returned her smile. But his soon flickered as he

looked out at the lake, sunrise struggling to break through the clouds of dawn.

"Hey, but you know . . . we might find—are you sure you really want to go?"

"Yes. And I'm aware of what could be out there. I won't turn back now."

It was preternaturally silent as the skiff glided along about the length of a basketball court from the shore. Some minutes later, pointing at the shore, Clay said, "I first saw him about here. I saw the lantern. Then I saw that he was carrying something over his shoulder. As I moved closer to the shore, I could see that it was a body. The body of a child."

"Could you tell . . . I mean . . . do you think it was a boy or a girl?"

"I'm pretty sure it was a girl. Long hair. I'm pretty sure the child had long hair."

Hillary nodded soberly.

"Little girls. They seem to be his target, don't they?"

"Yeah."

Clay shifted the pole to the other side of the boat and then said, "We'll put in here. This is where he had a boat tied down. He put the body in the boat and headed straight out."

It was a sandy, treeless jag of shore. On around to the left, trees, mostly pines, crowded close to the fog-shrouded water; in places their roots extended out slightly over the surface. A brushpile or two had formed in the backwash, and those piles ghosted through the fog.

"It's spooky," said Hillary.

"Ketch is spooky," Clay echoed.

They tied down the skiff and stood on the shore a moment, feeling the hauntingness of the scene close around them.

"Clay?"

"Yeah?"

"Do you . . . I mean, can you *see* anything?"

He was quiet for several seconds. Then he hunkered down and reached out to a patch of sand covered by foot-prints.

"I . . . you're going to think I sound like a coward, but I'm almost afraid to try."

She knelt down by him and hooked her arm around his elbow.

"No, Clay. I would never think that."

She leaned her head against his shoulder.

He cleared his throat.

"I promised Molly I would . . . I would do this. I just wish, you know . . . that I had some of her courage."

Hillary cupped her hand on his chin and kissed his ear and his cheek and then his lips.

"I'm here with you. We'll do this together."

He smiled and nodded and touched her hair.

"Okay, here goes."

He concentrated on the site where he had seen the boat depart. But all he saw was merely a filmy repeat of what he had seen already. When he pulled out of his imaging, Hillary said, "What did you see?"

"Nothing. Nothing new. Ketch and the body and the boat. Just like a photograph. That's all."

Hillary glanced around.

"What do we do now?"

"Let's walk along the shore. Maybe there'll be . . . I don't know. *Something.*"

Hand in hand they strolled along the shore, and anyone seeing them together would have thought of them as young lovers enjoying the early morning. But a closer look at their faces would have revealed a studied grimness.

Where the sandy shoreline dwindled, they began to negotiate the thicket and the crowding pines. They had gone fifty, then a hundred yards in silence before Clay said, "Maybe we should go back. I should take you home. I shouldn't be dragging you along on this craziness."

She punched at him gently. There was a tinge of aggravation in her voice.

"You didn't put a gun to my head, you know. I wouldn't be here if I didn't want to be—if I didn't want to be with you trying to solve the mystery."

"I'm not even sure what we're looking for."

Ten yards ahead, the bank angled up steeply before it cut away. Clay held Hillary's hand as she made her way up the incline then down to the edge of the water where a massive pine, its roots exposed, appeared to be growing out of nothing at all, suspended like a vision. Clay followed, slipping to his bottom, bouncing hard, and letting out a curse of pain.

Hillary giggled. Then she turned.

And suddenly her body stiffened. And she swung her hand to her mouth to stifle a scream.

Clay bumped in to her.

"Watch out. I'm seriously clumsy this morning," he exclaimed.

Her eyes glued to something beyond them, she squeezed his wrist and whispered, "Clay, look over there."

"Where?"

"Oh, my God," she whimpered, and then pushed herself

into his arms, her face in the hollow of his throat. She was trembling.

"Hillary, I still don't see—"

But then he did.

His breath caught. He blinked his eyes and let his breath out slowly.

"Damn," he muttered.

It was about thirty feet away.

A small body.

Seen from one angle it was rather like a fantasy—the caressing roots of the pine holding the child quite lovingly.

"Clay, oh, my God, my God!"

He held Hillary against him very tightly.

"Okay, okay . . . just . . . stay right here a moment."

Releasing her, he stepped forward, and as he did, he attempted to focus more clearly on details—the way the body was twisted, seemingly into an impossible position. It appeared deflated and gray.

But he could see reddish curls.

"Don't look at it again," he said to Hillary over his shoulder.

He crouched, stepped closer, and he realized that he, too, was trembling. The water was barely knee deep. But it felt unusually cold.

He stared at the body.

The color's all wrong.

The result of being in the lake all night? The gray. The color of the body gave the horror a completely different dimension.

He reached out. Behind him, he could hear Hillary crying softly.

He touched an arm.

And the jolt of surprise, followed by relief, made him stumble back, splashing.

"Clay? Clay, what is it?"

He gulped air for a few seconds before he could speak. His chest and throat burned. And his legs threatened to make him fall.

"Not . . . what . . . you think," he managed to say.

He composed himself.

Then he untangled the Raggedy Ann doll from the roots.

For five minutes or longer, Clay sat where the lake lapped onto the shore and held Hillary.

"He was carrying the doll," he said. "That's what I saw. But I thought . . . and now I wonder about something else."

"What?"

Having calmed herself as much as possible, Hillary searched his face as if it contained every answer to every question forming on her lips.

"Where's the boat? And where's Ketch?" said Clay.

Ten minutes later, they found the boat.

Waves gently rocking it, the boat was overturned, resting half out of the water another forty yards from where they had discovered the doll.

"Do you think he left it that way? Would Ketch leave it like that?"

Clay shook his head.

"Not likely. That boat washed to shore the same way the doll did. It must have capsized. If Ketch is a good swimmer . . ."

They had stopped short of the boat by fifteen or twenty feet. Hillary could see that Clay was staring at it, mesmerized by it as if it were some deadly creature which might raise itself and attack them.

"Tell me what it is," she said.

The fog had thickened. Visibility on the lake was virtually zero.

"I think . . . I'm going to know something if I . . ."

In her thoughts, she finished the sentence for him.

Touch it.

"Be careful," she said. But she wasn't certain why she said that. What danger could there be? There was no one else around. Just a boat that had washed onto the shore.

Am I afraid of Clay's imaging powers?

Yes. She admitted to herself that, in fact, she was.

And so was he.

"Well . . . here goes."

He marched to the boat and turned it right side up and pulled it all the way out of the water. It slid with a gritty, hissing noise.

Clay held the top rim of the boat with both hands.

For thirty seconds he hunkered there, silent and as still as stone.

When he pushed away from the boat and stood up, it was a violent movement, as if he were shaking free of an electrical wire which was shocking him.

"Damn," he murmured.

Hillary ran to him, hugging him around the waist. She waited for him to say something. And the moments seemed to stretch on, agonizing her.

"There was someone else," he said.

"What do you mean? Someone else in the boat? You didn't see anyone else last night, did you?" Then she hesitated before saying, "Was it the girl?"

"No."

She looked into his face; he was lost in thought.

"Tell me, Clay. What did you see?"

"I'm not real sure. There was someone . . . someone *larger* than Ketch. In the boat. The face was covered with—I don't know—like a black mask, maybe. I don't know. A man, I think. A large man. And I think I heard him say something. My imaging has never included that before."

She heard a ripple of fear in his voice.

"You heard the other man—not Ketch—it was the other man who said something?"

"Yeah. Listen . . . give me a second, okay? My head feels like somebody's stabbing knives in it."

Suddenly his knees buckled, and he fell forward. Hillary gasped and clutched at him.

"Clay? Oh, my God. Are you all right?"

"It'll pass. It always does."

She held him, tears stinging the corners of her eyes. Tears of fear and concern.

"Let's go back to my place," she whispered. "Clay, let's get away from here."

A minute later, with her help, Clay got to his feet. He turned and stared down at the boat.

"She wasn't being careful," he said.

Confused, Hillary moved around in front of him to meet his eyes.

"She? Clay, what is it?"

He shrugged.

"I . . . I have no idea. I mean, that's what the man said, I think. I think he said: 'She wasn't being careful,' but I don't know what he's talking about."

Sixteen

It was a little girl's voice.

"Shiver and quiver, little tree,/Silver and gold throw down over me."

The room was dark and very silent.

You could say nursery rhymes there, in that dark room, all day long and no one would hear you.

And no horrible flashes of light.

No burning.

No roars from unseen demons.

"Shiver and quiver, little tree . . ."

And you could pretend just about anything.

And be anyone else you wanted to be.

"Silver and gold throw down over me."

Because your father said it was okay.

But it was lonely. Down in that dark room.

Sometimes you need company.

Sometimes you have to go up and walk around. And be invisible.

And watch.

And strangle the voices in your head.

But sometimes you need someone to be with you. So you won't have to be by yourself.

"Shiver and quiver, little tree,/Silver and gold throw down over me."

It was a little girl's voice.

Seventeen

"So you're denying that any of this is true?"

Clay remained occupied with the bin of cantaloupes, sorting out those which were overly ripe. Katie Boyle's question hung in the air, and he could sense her impatience.

"Look, could you give me five minutes?" he said. "And then I'll be on break. I'll meet you at one of the benches in front of the store."

"All right, fine," she said. "I would appreciate it."

He watched her walk away, and so did the other guys working in the produce section. Boyle had a face and a figure that any young man would notice immediately. And immediately experience the pleasurable burn of sexual excitement.

But Boyle, as Hillary had suggested to him, "smelled a story"—she would be persistent. She wasn't there to charm him. She wanted information. And Clay knew that he would be forced to lie about his wild talent and about his suspicions regarding the Foxpath Fiend.

In the humid evening air, Clay and Boyle sat on a bench as cars moved desultorily in and out of the parking lot.

"They only give me ten minutes for a break," Clay explained.

Boyle, who had started her questions a few seconds after introducing herself earlier, nodded.

"My angle is simple," she began. "First I want to know whether you have some kind of psychic ability and then I want to hear what you know about the murder of Leigh Rybeck . . . and also your response to something I just heard about an hour ago."

Clay looked down at his hands, a gesture he realized would probably give him away. And the flashback he experienced was momentarily intense: reaching out for Ketch's boat, touching it, and sensing . . . someone. A large man.

She wasn't being careful.

"It's just gossip," he said. "When I was just a kid, well, yeah, a couple of things happened at school, and everybody thought I was . . . like the little boy in that book, *The Shining.* People believe what they wanna believe."

"Then it isn't true that you're trying to use some kind of paranormal power to help locate Leigh Rybeck's murderer?"

"Paranormal power?" He chuckled. "I have a vivid imagination sometimes, you know, but . . . that's about it."

"But you've been helping Hillary Garrett, haven't you? Have you two discovered anything other than what the police and other law enforcement officials already know?"

"I seriously doubt it."

"Are you and Hillary going together? Is this a romantic relationship?"

"Hey . . . I'm not gonna . . . our relationship is none of your business."

Clay could feel the back of his neck heating up.

Boyle smiled.

"Sorry, you're right. Okay, let's talk about the Foxpath Fiend."

"If you like."

"What makes you think he's the killer?"

Clay shrugged.

"I don't know that I do think that. But, you know, the guy's weird, and he's always in that area . . . you know, he hangs around up in the area of the old gold mine where they found that girl's body and . . ."

He held his tongue, but it was difficult.

Boyle was taking notes on a notepad.

"Donnie Ray Giles doesn't think the Foxpath Fiend is a suspect," she said.

"Well, he's got a right to his opinion."

"In fact, I was talking with him before I came here. We didn't get to talk long because he was on official business—at the county morgue."

Clay looked at her.

"Has there been . . . another murder?"

"A murder? Not according to Giles. But a body was found."

"At the lake?"

"Yes. Since you guessed that, maybe you can guess whose body it is."

"I have no idea."

He swallowed and felt hot needles in his throat.

"If your theory is right," she continued, "then the Foxpath Lake murders have come to an end."

"I'm not sure I'm following you. Whose body did they find?"

"Jeremy Ketch," she said. "The Foxpath Fiend."

"What . . . what happened to him?"

"According to Giles, he drowned."

* * *

She was trying hard to like it. But she honestly couldn't.

Her mother had listened to it outside Hillary's bedroom and had observed to her, with intentional irony, that such music could drive someone to drink. Charmian hated it as well. "I'll take Nat King Cole any day," she said. "He was a handsome man and could sing—a voice like hot chocolate on a cold night."

The guitar sounds twitched and the black man's voice grated and the lyrics made no sense to her. Something about "purple haze" and "kiss the sky." Disappointed, she ejected the tape.

"Sorry, Jimi Hendrix. You and I weren't meant for each other. But I hope Clay and I are."

She collapsed on the bed. Though it was late evening, she continued to feel tired from her morning escapade with Clay. The image of a sodden Raggedy Ann doll stuck in her thoughts like Velcro. Clay hadn't called her that afternoon. He would be getting off work soon, and she was anticipating hearing from him.

While she waited, she also thought about Dave Tanner. *Could he be a suspect?*

It seemed impossible.

And yet . . .

The twitter of the phone pulled her away from thoughts of Tanner.

"Hey, it's me. Can I see you tonight? I heard some weird news. We need to talk."

"Sure. I'll meet you down at the dock."

"Okay. Twenty minutes."

"Clay?"

"Yeah?"

"Oh . . . nothing. Nothing. I'll see you."

I love you.

That's what she had wanted to say. What she would say if she sensed the right moment. But she didn't want to risk scaring him off with an announcement of her feelings.

What if he doesn't love me?

After some touching up to her makeup and hair, she dashed to the dock and spread a blanket over the wooden planks. She was glad it was a clear night. Warm, and yet enough of a breeze that the humidity wasn't oppressive.

When she heard Clay poling the skiff toward the dock, she rubbed the pendant Molly had given her.

For good luck in love.

"Ahoy, there," he called out. "Would a stranger be welcome here?"

She laughed and waved.

"A handsome stranger, maybe."

"Sorry, ma'am. You'll have to take what comes floating your way."

In his arms she said, "Hmm, I think I got lucky."

He kissed her and touched her hair.

"So did I."

They sat on the blanket, and Hillary was pleasantly surprised that for a long run of seconds they gazed out onto the lake and said nothing, comfortable with the silence and with each other's presence.

Then Clay turned to her and said, "Katie Boyle caught up with me at Kroger's."

"I thought she might."

And with that, Clay recounted his conversation with the attractive young newspaper woman.

"She dropped a real bombshell at the end," he said.

Hillary waited. She could feel her body stiffen.

Clay continued.

"They found a body in the lake. Jeremy Ketch's. They're saying he drowned."

"You didn't say anything to Boyle about . . . what you saw, did you?"

"No, of course not."

"Clay, what are you thinking?"

He was staring out at the lake as if waiting for an answer to arise from its depths.

"Just that if the murders stop, we'll know we were probably right. That it was Ketch. And maybe one more thing: that maybe somebody made it *look* like Ketch drowned. *Somebody.*"

"But Clay . . . who? And why?"

He said nothing.

He continued staring at the lake.

Eighteen

The Fourth of July weekend, ushered in by hot, dry weather, brought a fresh infusion of visitors to Foxpath Lake for several days of boating and sunbathing and a nearly endless string of parties at the various cabins and homes which dotted the shoreline. At the center of the weekend tradition was a gigantic fireworks display hosted by the lake's business community, with the Foxpath Lake Marina being the launching pad for all the glittery bang. If the weather cooperated, you could see the display for miles and miles. During extended spells of dry weather, many area residents believed that the fireworks generated rain—something about breaking up the dome of high pressure which often settled itself over the South in summer.

Clay and Hillary chose to see the fireworks up close, though neither anticipated the event quite the same way they had as kids. It was a Saturday evening, and Hillary had parked her Pontiac in an ideal spot fronting the lake and not far from the Marina Grill. She and Clay were sitting on the front bumper, watching the crowd gather, watching people position lawnchairs and coolers, hearing them yell at their kids to stop chasing around, and hearing the twang of a country western band set up on a temporary stage right next to the lake.

"It's like nothing has happened," said Clay, scanning the crowd and all the eagerly pointless activity.

"What do you mean?"

Hillary slid closer and curled her hand inside his elbow.

"Well . . . Ketch drowning."

"But Clay, he wasn't exactly one of the community's leading citizens. I mean, he won't really be missed."

"That's not what I meant."

"I don't know what everybody else is thinking, but I'm relieved. When I woke up this morning, I thought, *it's over.* The Foxpath Fiend has drowned and that means there won't be another murder. And that little girl hasn't called again. We have the rest of the summer to enjoy."

"Maybe you're right. Maybe that's what we should do, enjoy the rest of the summer before putting the hammer down for school in the fall. We'll be seniors—the big cheeses."

He smiled, though Hillary could tell it was a forced smile.

"I'm ready to be a senior," she said, "but I'm not ready to face the future beyond that. College, I mean. I can't decide between broadcast journalism and education as possible majors. I really enjoyed my radio show, and maybe I'd like working in television. If I could do something with children—I love kids—something combining journalism and teaching . . . that would be ideal."

"You'll be good at whatever you choose."

"So will you. Your writing. You'll be able to develop your writing at college."

He shook his head.

"College . . . Hillary, there's no way I'd be able to afford to go to college."

"What do you mean? Of course there is. Haven't you ever heard of scholarships?"

"My grades aren't that good. And besides, now I feel even more obligated to look after my mother. College just isn't a real possibility for me."

Hillary started to disagree when she noticed that just beyond them, a few cars, someone was watching them intently.

"Clay . . . look over your shoulder. I get the feeling someone wants to keep an eye on us."

It was Giles. In uniform.

When Clay turned, Giles touched the brim of his hat, smiled, and then sauntered away.

"That guy gives me the creeps," said Clay. "Oh, and look who else is around."

Not twenty yards beyond Hillary was Katie Boyle, alone; she appeared to be interested in the parade of boats maneuvering for good vantage points from which to see the fireworks.

"She still smells a story, doesn't she?" said Hillary. "I feel like going over there and telling her to give it up—her story died when the Foxpath Fiend drowned."

"But did it?" Clay took her hand. "Come on. Let's leave your car here. I know a much better place for us."

From the skiff, and a quarter of a mile or so from any other boats, it seemed as if the fireworks display had been orchestrated exclusively for them. Relaxing and watching as the lake gently lapped against the skiff, they ooohed and aaahed like a couple of small children as each explosion of light and sound turned the night sky into a neon jangle.

Clay sat down behind Hillary and wrapped his arms around her waist and rested his chin on her shoulder.

"You're not cold, are you?"

She leaned back into the warmth of his chest.

"No. I'm fine. No, that's not quite right. I'm not just fine—I'm exactly where I want to be. With you."

He squeezed her more tightly.

"Wish I could be a lake bum again," he said. "And you could be one with me."

"A lake bum?"

"You know . . . just spend the whole summer, every day and every night, on and around the lake, just doing not much of anything. Living. Being free of all responsibility. Seeing as little of Kroger's as possible."

"You'd get tired of it. I mean, look at me. Unemployed. I'm feeling useless to society. I'm even tempted to see if they need help at the Marina Grill. I thought maybe I'd go in tomorrow and talk with George Smith at the station. Could be he needs a 'gopher.' I'd take anything."

Clay was silent for several seconds.

"You really believe it's over, don't you? That the mystery's been solved," he said.

She twisted around to face him.

"Hey, it was you who convinced me the killer was likely Ketch. Have you abandoned your own theory?"

The conclusion of the fireworks display was loud and fiery and filled the sky with artificial daylight. They held their ears, and when the cheer of the distant crowd and the car honks of approval had died, Clay let the darkness claim their spot again before saying, "Maybe I have. The lake's clear tonight. But it's not hard for me to imagine a mist rolling in and with it the ghost of Ketch trying to tell me something."

Rubbing her arms as if chilled, Hillary said, "Hey, this is an old trick—scaring your date so she'll snuggle up to you. You don't need to do it, you know. And since you've conjured up that ghost, what do you think it would be trying to tell you?"

Clay paused again. Hillary felt he was enjoying the moment.

"Oh, I don't know . . . a secret, maybe."

He reached for her, and she let him press her close.

Out farther on the lake, it appeared that something stirred, but neither Clay nor Hillary noticed it.

It wasn't the ghost of Jeremy Ketch, the Foxpath Fiend.

It was the shadow of a little girl.

Rising like the mists of dawn. And crying out in anguish.

Nineteen

Someone heard her.

Someone who had been watching the fireworks display.

The explosions of light. Horrible flashes of light.

Waiting for the burning to begin.

Because the dark and silent room couldn't protect you forever. And it was lonely down there.

Sometimes you needed company.

Sometimes you had to go up and walk around. And be invisible.

And remember what you'd seen.

And strangle the voices in your head.

And sometimes you needed someone to be with you. So you wouldn't have to be by yourself.

Because your father said it was okay.

Twenty

His mother's sobbing woke him.

It was the morning after the fireworks display, and Clay remembered that he had a debt to pay. He had traded a fellow worker his Saturday evening shift for an early Sunday morning shift. Still groggy, he threw on some clothes and went quietly to the door of his mother's room.

He knocked on it.

"Hey, you okay in there?"

The sobbing stopped.

He pushed open the door, and there she was, sitting on the edge of the bed in her robe, wisps of hair taking small flight and one streaking across her cheek where tears had plastered it to her skin.

At the sight of Clay, his mother smiled and blinked her eyes in the shadows.

"Did I wake you up?" she asked.

He went to her and knelt in front of her. He couldn't recall ever seeing her look so old. And so miserable.

"I had to get up anyway. I've got the morning shift. Got to get those bananas and those heads of lettuce out where folks can look them over."

"Did you get to see the fireworks?"

"Yeah . . . Hillary Garrett and I saw them. They were nice, but I always think they could use the money on something else. It's kinda like seeing dollar bills exploding."

"Oh, I don't know about that," said his mother, looking somewhere just above him. "Folks need some . . . some color and noise in their lives. Some, anyways."

"Maybe so."

"You know . . . our Molly, she . . . she sure loved those fireworks every year. She . . ."

Her voice trailed off and more tears threatened.

"Yeah. Yeah . . . Molly loved fireworks."

His mother folded her hands in her lap and sighed.

"The reason I've been crying," she began, "is 'cause I'm feeling . . . oh, some of it's 'cause I miss our little Molly. There's that. And I do. I do miss her. But it's bein' lonely, mostly. Not that you're not good company. You are. And good to help with everything while your father's not here. I'm lonely in a different way . . . and I've been thinkin' about doin' something."

Clay waited a moment for her to continue. When she didn't, he said, "About doing what?"

"Oh, it's probably not . . . oh, nothing."

She waved him away.

He hugged her and then met her eyes.

"I'll take care of you," he said. "You know I will. But I've got to hustle off to work right now. You need anything at the store?"

She shook her head.

"No. No, I'm halfway, you know . . . halfway expectin' your father to call this morning. I just have a feelin' he will."

Blinking away a surge of frustration, Clay turned and left the room as quietly as he had entered it.

At work, he forced thoughts of his mother aside. He believed he knew what she wanted to do. With summer's end, some decisions would have to be made. For the moment, however, he wanted to think about anything else. About something much more pleasant.

Like Hillary.

As he arranged a new shipment of white grapes, he thought about how much he enjoyed holding her. He enjoyed the fragrance of her, the taste of her lips; her touch was loving and just restrained enough and warm enough to make him always want her close. He had grown to like her voice, to like the seriousness of its tone.

But we don't like many of the same things.

It was true. Their tastes in music and movies, books and clothes seemed miles apart at times. They weren't interested in many of the same ideas or political or cultural issues. What was it, then? What had brought them together?

The answer seemed obvious enough.

Molly.

Molly and "Just Pretend" and the murder of Leigh Rybeck. And his imaging ability—that was a factor, too. In short, a mysterious sequence of events had brought them together.

But the mystery's been solved.

Or has it?

He swam through the remainder of his shift, surrendering to thoughts and images of Jeremy Ketch—the drowning (*alleged* drowning)—and the flash of something experienced in touching Ketch's boat.

She wasn't being careful.

"Ketch didn't drown," he whispered to himself as he

tossed off his apron and went to punch out around noon. "Somebody murdered him. But I don't know why. Or who."

Instead of going home, he decided to pedal to Hillary's. He wanted to try out a new theory which was coalescing in his thoughts. He planned to stop along the way at the Quik Shoppe for a soft drink.

When he wheeled into the parking lot, he immediately braked.

"Whoa," he murmured. "What kinda trouble have we here?"

There were two police cars, one sheriff's department car, and Donnie Ray Giles's patrol car. No customers were being allowed in the front door, so Clay sneaked around behind. At the rear of the store, Ed Newton, its owner, had built a small bait shop with steps leading down from it to a dock and boat rental area.

From the angle of his vantage point, Clay could see two officers talking with Newton, a heavyset man whose daughter had married the Foxpath High basketball coach, Sid Lightner. Newton looked extremely distraught. Clay knew it was something serious—he guessed a robbery.

He glanced around and was about to leave, hoping Hillary might have some details on whatever incident had taken place, when he noticed a man standing alone on the dock, staring out into the bright glare of the lake.

It was John Jaggery.

"That's all I know."

Jaggery seemed uncomfortable. But Clay reasoned that,

given the circumstances, such discomfort was understandable.

"Then she's been missing since last night?" said Clay.

Jaggery took a large, red handkerchief out of the back
pocket of his jumpsuit and dabbed at his sweaty forehead.

"Apparently she had come down here after the fireworks to get some little toy she had left—she never came
back. That's what Mr. Giles told me. I suppose that anything he would tell me about the case is not confidential
information. I suppose you'll tell Hillary about this."

"She'll be interested and concerned, especially since
there might be a link between this and—"

"No reason to think there is," said Jaggery. "Likely it's
a simple case of drowning. Oh, they've searched along
here for the body, but it's very possible it drifted out.
They'll find it when they make a more exhaustive search."

"Poor Mr. Newton and his wife must feel horrible,"
said Clay. "Taking care of their only grandchild and something like this happens. They'll never forgive themselves."

Jaggery appeared lost in some inner landscape, and yet
Clay was surprised to discover that he wasn't.

"But you have to," he said. "You have to forgive yourself because . . . you can't control everything." He was
clenching his fists. "It tears at you, but you can't control
things like this. You can't always keep the people you love
safe."

Clay listened and suddenly recalled hearing how deeply
Jaggery had been grieving from the loss of his wife.

And then, without saying good-bye or anything more,
Jaggery walked away. Clay watched him ascend the steps
where he was met by Donnie Ray Giles.

For nearly a minute Clay leaned against the dock railing

and let Jaggery's account of the situation tumble over and over in his thoughts: Christina Lightner, age seven, daughter of Sid and Marcee Lightner, was missing.

Drowned?

Clay closed his eyes and ran his fingers along the railing. He hunkered down and touched the planks and felt dizzy. Shadows paraded behind his eyes. And he thought he heard a little girl's voice. But at first, no distinct words. Then . . . something.

A nursery rhyme?

He stood up so suddenly that his knees nearly gave out.

Yes, he could hear faint echoes of that voice.

He knew that rhyme.

And he knew one thing more.

Christina Lightner had not drowned.

"Picking up any vibrations?"

Katie Boyle surprised him. He turned, and her pretty face carried a mixed expression—haughtiness and fierceness.

"From the heat, yeah," said Clay. He was proud of himself for the verbal comeback. And it was true. The east Alabama day was heating up, promising to be in the 90s.

Her ever present notebook pressed to her breasts, she stepped down onto the dock.

"Mr. Giles and the other officers aren't saying much. They plan to drag this area of the lake this afternoon, but my intuition says they don't really believe the Lightner girl drowned. Any theories of your own, Mr. Brannon?"

"None. I'm just sorry for Mr. Newton and his wife and, of course, for Coach Lightner and his wife. I know what it feels like to lose someone you love. I think I know some of what they're going through."

Boyle was close to him, and yet something in her voice was distant and calculating.

"We can't blame *this* on the Foxpath Fiend, can we?"

"Not unless he has a real active ghost."

"What could have happened to that little girl? Did she just wander off into the woods? Is she out there somewhere lost and very tired and hungry?"

Clay shrugged. The chill of Boyle's tone was unsettling.

"That's a possibility. It would be easy to do, though I assume they've been combing the woods around."

"About every square inch of the immediate area. So now they suspect a drowning. But you don't believe she drowned, do you?"

The impact of her penetrating stare caused him to look away.

"I don't believe anything one way or another. Lots of different things could have happened."

"You don't believe the Foxpath Fiend drowned either, do you?"

"Hey . . . what is this? Giles found the body. Apparently there was an investigation—they say he drowned, so who am I to go against that?"

Boyle smiled knowingly.

"You're right," she smirked. "Who are you to go against the official ruling—even if you know the truth?"

"Who says I know the truth?"

Boyle began to walk away, then slowed, and over her shoulder she said, "My intuition does."

Clay shook his head in exasperation and puzzlement. *She's not giving up.*

After watching Boyle disappear up the steps to the bait shop, he began to negotiate the thicket along the shoreline. He forced aside further thoughts of Boyle and continued moving, quickly at first, then slowing because . . .

He came this way.

He? Yes.

Against the sting of sweat rivulets, Clay closed his eyes. He peeled off his T-shirt and squatted down so that he could touch the shoreline, its loose sand and scattered pinestraw.

Someone struggling.

The barely audible sound of a child crying. A child whose mouth was covered. A child who was terrified.

This way.

Clay could feel every nerve in his body; they were scurrying like ants after their mound has been disturbed. He followed the trail, and it was like following . . . shadows.

He followed those shadows eagerly, at times almost unconsciously, never quite fully aware of where he was until he reached the old gold mine area.

He entered one of the caves. The cool air should have been refreshing, but it wasn't. Because . . . suddenly he could see pencil-thin, gray outlines of them.

A man and a girl.

He approached the outlines.

And they dissolved.

For nearly a minute, he lost the image of them. Waves of nausea swept over him; his head roared and he was having difficulty breathing.

His imaging was turning upon him like some invisible force, like something from one of the "Star Trek" reruns he and Molly used to watch.

Except that this was real.

Very real.

Outside the cave he felt slightly better.

He closed his eyes again and began to image the movement of the man and the girl.

A little girl in extreme danger.

But is it Christina Lightner?

He had no way of being certain.

Just as he had no clear idea of who her abductor was.

The new trail led him down to the shore again, to a spot just beyond where he kept his father's skiff tied. He looked for footprints but found nothing distinct.

He concentrated upon the scene.

They got in a boat here.

Of that much he was reasonably certain.

He stood looking out at Foxpath Lake. It loomed there, huge, with a shoreline which stretched for miles. Tracing the images of a man and a girl in a boat on such a large lake seemed a hopeless, even crazy task.

He wished Hillary could be with him. He needed her support.

He untied the skiff and pushed off, and though he felt very weak—his stomach knotted and his head swimming in pain—he knew that he had to try to follow the ghostly residues which seemed to tug at him as if he were tethered to them by a supernatural rope.

Through the afternoon heat and the razor-like glare of the sun upon the surface, he poled the skiff deliberately, keeping his wild talent activated. His mouth was parched and he often had to mop sweat from his face, but he continued.

They went this way.

And there's a good chance no one saw them.

Everyone would have had their attention drawn to the fireworks display. The man who had abducted young Christina had picked an ideal moment.

When Clay had poled to within sight of Hillary's house, he nearly stopped to get her, but then he recalled that she had planned to go to the radio station this afternoon. And besides that . . . he suddenly needed to be alone with his imaging.

Because it was getting stronger.

The ghostly path of the man and the girl in the boat opened wider. Clay was as sure as he could be that they had come this way.

A quarter of a mile farther and disappointment.

The images faded within thirty yards of the next dock.

Damn it, where'd you go? Where'd you take her?

Confused, angered, he guided his skiff to the dock; he was almost too weak to tie down.

Have I lost them?

He decided to rest. He pulled himself up onto the wooden planks of the dock and ran his fingers along the somewhat splintery surface of one plank.

And the image of the man and the girl, just for an instant, materialized.

Is this where he took her?

For a minute or longer, Clay stared at the house at the far end of the line of steps.

But it can't be.

My God, no.

And yet the images had flowed toward that house.

"Hillary," he whispered, "oh, my God. You're not going to believe this."

* * *

Hillary couldn't believe how well her visit to the station had gone. Her twenty minute conversation with George Smith had been laced with warmth and friendliness. Smith, the "Just Pretend" controversy behind him, was in high spirits, and though he couldn't promise anything, he suggested several ways in which Hillary might easily assume a role at the station once again—and perhaps another shot at an "on air" program.

So it was that with a smile on her face, Hillary stuck her head in the broadcasting booth from which "Just Pretend" had originated. She experienced a wave of nostalgia and a sprinkle of regret, but mostly her associations were good ones. And it was not that she completely repressed a certain phone call she had received on air—no, that, of course, remained quite alive in her memory—rather, it was that she looked to a favorable forecast regarding the future.

The future looked bright.

I have my whole life ahead of me. And I have Clay.

"Hey, the ghost haunts her former abode."

Hillary wheeled around to face Dave Tanner. Her breath caught, and then she smiled, but not as warmly as she might have weeks ago.

"Oh, hi . . . everything looks the same," she said. The image of Tanner and the little girl at the phone booth knifed through her thoughts. She knew her nervousness was showing.

"But everything isn't the same. In fact . . . nothing's the same since you've been gone."

He stepped closer, and she found herself making a countering step back.

"Your boss says things are running smoothly."

Tanner appeared not to be listening. He was looking at her as if he wanted to devour her.

"I've been meaning to call you," he said. "I've wanted to go out with you from the day I first saw you."

Hillary shrugged self-consciously.

"Well, I've been keeping busy."

Not entirely a lie. She wanted to brush him off, but she was feeling a curious fear rising within her.

What kind of guy is this?

Suddenly she didn't know. Her imagination was painting a very dark portrait.

"Too busy to take in a movie or—"

The crackle of a little girl's laughter flooded the hallway outside the booth. Beyond Tanner, Hillary could see the girl bouncing along, laughing, then punching playfully at Tanner.

"Dave, when are we goin' for ice cream, huh? You said it would be just a minute, and a minute's up. So come on and let's go."

"Hey, spook," said Tanner. He pulled the girl against his hip and leaned down and kissed her on top of her head.

"Hillary, this is Michelle, my older sister's kid. I've been sorta babysitting while my sister and her husband are in Mexico. And I've got to tell ya, this kid is a mess— she wears me out. But her parents are coming home tomorrow and my sentence'll be over."

Hillary smiled at the little girl.

The same little girl she had seen Tanner with at the phone booth.

She felt as if she owed Tanner an apology.

She felt a surge of relief.

And to the girl she said, "Hi, Michelle. Is Dave a pretty good uncle?"

"When he buys me ice cream, yeah he's the best!"

Twenty-one

Later Hillary would wonder why she hadn't heard about the Lightner girl. Had neither George Smith nor Dave Tanner been aware of the missing child?

From the station, Hillary had gone to the Village Mall to do some shopping. It was nearing 5:00 when she returned, greeted by Charmian who explained that Mr. Garrett had called and was flying home early from a consulting job. Hillary's mother was driving to Atlanta to meet him.

Hillary was pleasantly surprised.

"Maybe it's a good sign," she said to Charmian.

"I hope you be right," said Charmian. "I surely do."

Charmian had one more thing to say: "You got you a visitor waitin' on the deck. I gave him some lemonade. He sure do wanna see you."

It was Clay.

She ran to him and kissed him, and before he could utter more than a greeting she had launched into an account of her day: the visit with George Smith, the discovery concerning Dave Tanner, and the potentially positive implications of her mother driving to the airport to pick up her father.

Hillary was on a high.

And that made Clay reluctant—very reluctant—to burst

her bubble. He couldn't just pretend that everything was seashells and balloons. He was carrying around dark news, news he would have to share with her.

"I don't have to be a mindreader," she said, "to see that your day hasn't been as good as mine."

He looked away, then back at her. He seemed to be studying her face like someone might study a wall of hieroglyphics.

"You haven't heard, have you?"

"I . . . no, I mean . . . heard what?"

The somber cast of his eyes frightened her.

"It's not over," he said.

And she knew instantly what he meant. She pressed her fingers to her mouth.

"What's happened?"

"Christina Lightner, the coach's daughter . . . she's missing."

"Missing?"

Clay recounted what he knew, leaving out a few details—such as his conversations with John Jaggery and Katie Boyle. He didn't mention where his imaging had taken him. And when he had finished, Hillary said, "And you don't think she drowned, do you?"

The echo of Boyle's words struck him.

He shook his head.

"I've got something to tell you," he continued, "that's going to be real hard for you to believe—it's hard for me to believe."

She felt as if someone were spinning and spinning her around with no intention of ever stopping the spinning.

"What? What is it? Did you see something? Did someone . . . did you *see* someone take her?"

"Yeah."

"Who? And where was she taken? Is she . . . has she been harmed?"

"I don't know how she is. I'm not sure what to do because it's such a serious accusation . . . and I have no proof—only what the imaging produced."

Folding her hands in her lap, Hillary tried to calm herself, tried to prepare herself for the details of what Clay saw.

"I want to know," she said.

"Okay. But remember—I warned you. What I have to tell you is a real bad scene."

He narrated events up to the point at which the man and the girl disappeared, and there he hesitated.

Hillary's mind was racing.

"So the man must have taken her right by here. And so she could be somewhere close. Did you recognize that dock and the house?"

Clay continued to hesitate. Then he reached out for her hand and said, "Yeah, I know them. The dock and the house—they're John Jaggery's."

Hillary felt as if someone had violently thrust a hot branding iron against her, high on her chest. Mentally, emotionally, she was reeling. She was speechless. Incredulous. And, most of all, feelings of intense anger and hurt were rising within her.

She stared at Clay.

She could not believe that he had made such a cruel accusation. And her only thought was that she never wanted to see him again.

* * *

The next day Clay worked the morning shift, though "work" would not be an accurate description of the manner in which he went about his duties in the produce department of Kroger's. He was merely "putting in his time," ghosting through the minutes in a daze.

He tried twice to call Hillary.

Both times Charmian told him she did not want to come to the phone. He knew there was no point in leaving a message—*what message would I leave?*—and there wasn't much chance she would return his call.

While he had anticipated that she would respond negatively to what his imaging suggested, he had not been prepared for the degree of her defensiveness.

It felt like the death of their relationship.

What would Molly say to me about now?

My God, I miss you, Queen Mab.

After work—or rather, after completing his shift—he pedaled up to the lake. It was hot, and the forecast called for late afternoon or early evening thundershowers, some possibly severe. The dome of high pressure was about ready to break; typically, when it did, the weather tended to get nasty.

His meandering took him from the Quik Shoppe to the Children's Graveyard. He felt miserable. And he felt helpless. Part of him wanted to tell Hillary to forget everything he had said about his most recent imaging—that it was a mistake, that he had tried again and the shadows had not led to John Jaggery's. He wanted to.

But he couldn't.

He had seen Christina Lightner once or twice, a darling little girl with pitch-black hair and eyes. Innocently beautiful.

What terror is she going through right this moment?
Guilt tore at him with shark's teeth.

He knew that at the very least he should share his information with the authorities, though he doubted they would believe him. He also knew that if he had sufficient courage he would go to Jaggery's and rescue the girl.

But what if my imaging is wrong?

It was definitely a possibility.

He would look foolish.

He would lose Hillary forever.

But what if you could save a little girl's life?

John Jaggery.

He tried to imagine the retired school counselor as a child killer. It was rather like trying to imagine Foxpath Lake dry as a bone. And yet, weren't there stories of mild-mannered individuals with a dark, private side, a psychopathic side? Did such a narrative fit Jaggery?

Or was someone else involved?

"You're not in here robbin' graves, are ya?"

Donnie Ray Giles had approached so silently that Clay had not heard him.

"Oh . . . man, you scared the—you should have coughed or something."

Giles, in full uniform, was sweating profusely. He took off his hat and fanned himself. As he talked, he let his eyes roam around the graveyard and the encroaching woods.

"You know Foxpath Lake pretty good, doncha?"

Clay shrugged.

"Pretty well, yeah."

Giles nodded.

"You like comin' to this graveyard, do ya?"

"My sister and I used to come here all the time. Yeah, it's peaceful. A good place to think things over."

"You got somethin' troubling your mind, do ya?"

"Could be, sure. Personal stuff."

"Uh-huh, I see . . . I see. Well, maybe this'd be a good place for me, too, 'cause I've got some things troubling my mind. You wanna hear what they are?"

Clay chuckled nervously.

"I have a feeling I'm going to have to hear them whether I want to or not."

"No, sir. No, sir, that's not so. I'm not officially detainin' you. Just, you might say, sharin' my thoughts. Nothin' wrong with that, is there?"

"I guess not."

"Here's the ticket," said Giles, meeting Clay's eyes directly. Giles had stopped fanning. "That Lightner girl didn't drown. Somebody took her. Now, it wasn't Jeremy Ketch, 'cause Ketch is buried up behind his mama's shack. Wasn't him. And it wasn't no drifter, I'm supposin', like I thought mebbe it was before." He paused and looked up at the sky as if something had suddenly drawn his attention. Then he said, "I'm havin' to rack my brain for new suspects. Any reason why I shouldn't suspect you?"

Clay could feel his jaw tightening. He knew that he was about to lose his cool.

"Not a one," he said. "Seems you could suspect about anyone who lives up here at the lake. Any reason why people shouldn't suspect you, Mr. Giles?"

His face flushing, Giles leaned over and spit to one side. When he looked at Clay again he was smiling.

"It'd be a sad commentary if people suspected the very men assigned to protect 'em."

"That it would. Tell that to Ed Newton. Tell it to Coach Lightner and his wife. Who was protecting their daughter?"

"Well, sir, I know exactly the problem 'bout their daughter. I know what likely happened."

"I would be interested to hear that," said Clay.

"Aw right, aw right, I'll tell you. It's as simple as this: that little girl . . . she wasn't being careful."

Hillary hadn't cried as much since Chad Gillis asked Shandra Pickney to the eighth grade graduation dance instead of her. At that time Hillary had made a secret pact with herself never to get so torn up over a guy.

But Clay was different.

But he's wrong.

To suggest that John Jaggery was even remotely involved with the summer horrors which had visited Foxpath Lake was as wrongheaded as she could imagine.

In her room, sprawled on her bed, Hillary listened to her radio and thought hard about what she should do. She hated not returning Clay's calls, and yet he had so angered her that she couldn't bring herself to want to communicate with him.

Evening was approaching, and her dad had stuck his head in to say that he and Hillary's mother had been invited to the home of some friends across the lake. He seemed in a good mood. Were her parents going to be able to fix what was broken? Or were they merely going through the motions of one last, but ultimately futile, attempt to repair their marriage?

Hillary told him to have a good time and, like a parent,

cautioned him to watch the weather. There was distant thunder. Then, around 6:00, she received the first call.

A little girl's voice.

"Help me."

Hillary struggled to generate a dialogue, to get any information that might make a difference. But her efforts were too eager, too laced with anxiety.

The caller hung up.

And fifteen minutes later, called again.

A little girl's voice.

"Help me."

"Please, please," said Hillary. "I want to help. Tell me where you are . . . *please.*"

"Come help me.

The buzz of the dial tone was suddenly deafening.

Hillary knew that she had to do something. She had to leave the house.

And there was only one place she could think of to go to.

Twenty-two

Sitting in John Jaggery's cozy living room, Hillary relaxed. The anxieties generated by the little girl's calls and by Clay's veiled accusation about Jaggery were dissolving by the minute as she engaged in conversation with her dear friend.

Clay's wrong.

His imaging failed him this time.

Thunder boomed across the lake just as Jaggery was explaining to Hillary about Bermuda grass not growing well in shade.

"Oh, my, would you listen to that," he said. "I can't complain, though, we need the rain." Then he smiled and changed the subject. "And how is that dear Miss Charmian these days?"

"Fine. The heat bothers her. I worry about her getting home these evenings—she's been driving that old beat up yellow Pinto. Hope she makes it home before the storm hits."

"And your folks—what's the latest word there?"

Hillary beamed. She couldn't suppress the optimism in her tone.

"Things look much better. They're going out together this evening. To visit friends. The atmosphere around home has improved. Maybe they're about to turn a corner—who can say? I feel good about them. Maybe I shouldn't get my hopes up too high, but I'm going to cling to every positive sign at this point. If Mom can just admit her problem and go in for some help, then I think they've got a chance. Dad can help a lot if he'll encourage her and support her. We'll see."

"Oh, that's wonderful news," said Jaggery. "I'll keep my fingers crossed—I will."

There was more thunder and a brilliant stroke or two of lightning. Evening settled heavily upon the lake, and Jaggery's small living room seemed to attract more and more shadows. But Hillary didn't mind. She was comfortable. Her mind much more at ease.

"I'm glad they can go out evenings and not have to worry about getting a babysitter for me. And I like having my freedom, too. Freedom to come and go as I please."

"But they'll be concerned about you . . . I mean, with this storm brewing. You left them a note saying where you'd be, didn't you?"

Hillary shook her head.

"No reason to. I knew I'd be back before they called it an evening. Besides, if I'm not at home, they'll assume I'm with Clay."

"Oh, yes. Yes, of course. You have, indeed, become an independent young woman. And now, approaching your final year of high school—it seems just yesterday that you were a wet-behind-the-ears freshman. Where does the time go?"

Hillary giggled.

"I can't believe how innocent I was back then. Good thing I had a great counselor."

She reached across the coffee table and patted the back

of his hand. When he smiled at her she suddenly noticed how tired he looked. Old and wrinkled and stressed around the eyes.

"Heavens, thanks . . . you're an angel," he said.

"Well, perhaps I should be going. I just wanted to see how you are, and so I—"

"It shows, doesn't it?"

"It? I . . . what do you mean?"

He smiled and coiled his hands together as if they were large pieces of rope.

"The days are . . . difficult," he murmured.

Hillary felt her breathing shift roughly. Out on the lake the wind gusted ahead of the approaching thunderstorm.

"You miss your wife, don't you?" she said. "That's understandable. But I think you've handled the loss very well."

"I do miss Velma, and now there's so much these days . . . things I . . . can't really deal with. Life moves so strangely. And so very quickly. The days . . . I wish sometimes that I could freeze time. Stop it the way . . . the way a photo stops it."

He gestured beyond her, and she turned in her chair to glance at a floor-to-ceiling bookcase lined with photos.

"You have a marvelous assortment of photos," she said. The sudden emergence of Jaggery's somber mood gave an unsettling edge to the moment. She got up and strolled to the bookcase.

"Miss Velma was certainly a beautiful woman." Pointing at one of the photos, Hillary asked, "How old were you when this was taken?"

The photo showed a young man and young woman in collegiate sweaters smiling from the front seat of a convertible. Jaggery made his way to the bookcase and smiled wistfully.

"Old enough to believe we understood all we needed to about life. Early 20s, I suppose. I thought Velma was the most beautiful woman on the planet."

"These photos show your entire life, don't they?"

"They show the surface of it . . . only the surface."

"Here are some of your son Bill—is he feeling better lately?"

"Bill takes care of himself. Being in the military made him that way."

Hillary picked up a photo capturing the son in full combat gear.

"He was in Desert Storm, wasn't he?"

"Yes. Velma and I were quite proud of him. He takes care of himself now."

"Oh, here's a side of you I didn't know about." Hillary laughed softly at a photo showing Jaggery, baseball cap on sideways, being mobbed by ten or twelve little girls.

Jaggery smiled at the sight of it.

"The 'Lionettes'—a girls' softball team sponsored by the Foxpath Lion's Club. First time they had ever sponsored a girls' team. I adored those little gals. Wish I could've taken every one of them home with me, but Velma would have thrown a fit. Billy, too. We only won two games that year, but we had exceptional team spirit."

Holding another photo which she was examining closely, Hillary said, "Isn't this . . . this is someone I know, isn't it?"

At her shoulder, Jaggery squinted.

"Oh, of course, you do. It's Donnie Ray Giles."

Hillary couldn't keep from laughing.

"But he looks . . . so sad. How old was he? Not more than fifteen or sixteen, was he?"

The photo framed Giles sitting on a concrete picnic bench. He wasn't smiling. There was misery in his eyes.

"Something like that," said Jaggery. "He spent quite a bit of time with Velma and me one summer. We often thought of him rather like a second son. I'm pleased that he has a position now. Some authority. It gives him some identity."

"He and I don't hit it off," Hillary confessed. "I'm not sure what it is . . . he's . . . seems like he's suspicious of me for some reason."

"He had a troubled childhood. He's not an easy fellow to get to know, and, well, like everyone else, there's a side to him no one knows."

"I'm not among those who wants to know."

"He's not a bad fellow. Actually, he's quite knowledge-able of Foxpath Lake. Knows the secrets of the area." Jaggery paused to chuckle to himself. "Oh, Donnie Ray's just misunderstood. If he's your friend, he'll do anything for you. Take, well . . . for example, he helped me build on to my cabin last summer—a sub-basement area. He made it tight as a tick. Donnie Ray's okay."

"Do you think he's a good shore patrolman?"

Jaggery chuckled again.

"Good enough. What I mean is, he's certainly capable of handling most of what occurs on or around the lake. This summer, unfortunately, has been a different story. The murder of the Rybeck girl and the drowning of Jeremy Ketch . . . and now this terrible business of the Lightner girl . . . no, I'm afraid he's out of his league. I'm afraid he . . ."

As his voice trailed off, Hillary sat down again. Jaggery remained standing. He appeared restless and uneasy.

"Mr. Jaggery, what did you know about Jeremy Ketch?"

She thought Jaggery had not been listening, but almost immediately he broke from his speculative reverie and said, "I know he didn't kill the Rybeck girl. And . . . I regret that he couldn't have lived out his days more peacefully. He and Donnie Ray were sorta buddies at one time. Oh, Jeremy Ketch was a poor soul, tortured at times, locked in a desperate fight to stay sane."

"Clay doesn't think he drowned."

Hillary's comment escaped from her lips before she considered its potential impact. She found herself holding her breath, anticipating Jaggery's response.

Slowly, quite deliberately, Jaggery raised a hand and rested it against the bookcase. He patted it as if to test how substantial it was.

"Clay Brannon doesn't think Jeremy Ketch drowned—then what, I wonder, does he assume happened instead?"

"He's . . . not sure. This 'imaging' ability he has, well, he used it along the shore, where he had seen Ketch push off into the lake in a boat. And he *saw* something. Someone else with Ketch. He doesn't believe Ketch drowned."

Jaggery was silent. It was the kind of silence which changes the atmosphere in a room. Hillary felt that even the shadows had changed, enlarged, grown more threatening. Thunder vibrated the walls.

Why am I feeling so spooked?

She was irritated at herself for getting into Clay's imaging. Clearly, it was unreliable. And she was puzzled by her reaction to Jaggery's silence. She was feeling like a little girl who fears a bogeyman under her bed.

Jaggery drew himself up quite straight and tall and said, "I wish you weren't seeing Clay Brannon."

"Why? Why . . . do you say that?"

He went and sat down opposite her and smiled. His manner changed completely.

"I'm sorry. Forgive me, dear. I have absolutely no right to say such a thing. While you are my friend, and I admire you without reservation, I shouldn't attempt to intrude upon your personal life—such comments are vestiges of my role as a counselor. They're out of line. Please forget that I said anything."

"It's all right. You're acting as a friend and wanting what's best for me. In this case, it's just that I don't believe you know Clay. Oh, I'm upset with him at the moment, but I do care very much for him . . . he's . . . so different from most of the guys I know. I wish you and he—"

"Ah, you wish—what a magical notion—*wishing*. I have many wishes these days. 'Shiver and quiver, little tree/Silver and gold throw down over me.' "

Hillary gasped.

"You know that line, too. I learned it from Clay."

Jaggery's smile flickered.

"It's the kind of line which stays with you. Something your mental filter picks up, and a little voice in some quiet cell of your thoughts repeats it over and over again. We need wishes. What is *your* fondest wish, my dear?"

"Selfish wishes jump into my mind, but the one this evening I most want to come true is about Christina Lightner: I wish I knew that she was safe. Someone has taken her—I just feel that's what's happened—someone has taken her, and if she's still alive, then she's experiencing a nightmare. And I can't imagine what's going on in the mind of any person who would prey upon a child."

Jaggery looked away thoughtfully. When he spoke, his tone was serious again, and this time it also possessed another quality—something eerie, like the tone of a voice in a vacated house.

"Such a person . . . no longer has a will of his own."

"A psychotic, you mean? But why must they hurt someone who's so innocent?"

"You assume they have a choice."

"Oh, this is a dreadful topic." Hillary paused and gripped her elbows and shuddered. She attempted to smile, hoping to find a smooth transition into another subject.

And that's when Jaggery surprised her.

"You've gotten more calls, haven't you?"

"More. . . . I don't know what . . ."

But she did. She knew instantly what he was referring to. She started to stand up, but he gestured for her to remain seated.

"I don't have an explanation, not a good one at least, of what's going on," said Jaggery. "The only way I can explain it to myself is to say that sometimes a person, an otherwise sane person, experiences a total mental disruption. Like a fire in the brain. A fire that he fights . . . but can't extinguish."

Hillary could feel her heart beating in her throat.

"But Jeremy Ketch is the only person around the lake who appeared to be that way. So why has . . ."

Jaggery cleared his throat and whispered, "Appeared."

Hillary laughed nervously.

Rain began to tap on the roof, sweeping in behind a fresh round of thunder and lightning.

"A perfect night to talk about such weird stuff, but I really better get on home before it starts raining harder."

Jaggery raised his hand, palm out.

"Yes, we're scaring each other like school kids. But I do have one question for you, Hillary, and it's about Clay."

"What is it?"

"I assume he used his—'imaging,' you call it?—his ability to trace the Lightner girl. May I ask what he discovered?"

"You may—it's crazy, though. It's why I'm mad at him. I mean, for even thinking that it might involve . . . okay, here's what he claims." She took a deep breath. "He says he *saw* a man take the Lightner girl in a boat and they docked . . . they docked at *your* dock . . . and disappeared into *this* house. I told him he's wrong, of course. I shouldn't have gotten so sucked in to what he thinks he's seen. Because, in this case, he's wrong."

Jaggery nodded.

He rose and walked over to the bookcase. Thunder generated a deep hum throughout the house.

"Well," he said. Hillary sensed that the man felt somehow relieved. "The storm is much too heavy for you to leave at this time."

"If you don't mind," she said, "I'll just wait it out."

"Wait it out? Yes. Yes, of course." Suddenly he reached for a switch on the wall and stepped away from the bookcase as the entire unit swung away to reveal a dark block of a room about the size of a small closet.

Puzzled, Hillary stared at it. She looked at Jaggery for an explanation.

There was an expression of deep sadness on his face.

"The storm's going to get much worse," he said, "and so now, that means . . . you'll have to stay."

On legs which threatened not to support her, Hillary stood up. She could hear a voice, and it seemed to be coming from the closet. Or *below* the closet.

A little girl's voice.

Twenty-three

Donnie Ray Giles looked as if he'd seen a ghost.

Because he had.

Two of them, in fact.

As he sat at the counter of the Foxpath Lake Marina Grill and stirred cream into his coffee, he listened to the rain beat against the roof, and when the lightning flashed he tried to focus upon the surface of the lake.

To see whether they were out there.

Whether they had followed him. Were stalking him.

Earlier, at twilight, before the storm unleashed its fury, he had seen them. He had been walking along the shore below the old gold mine, just thinking. Thinking very hard. About a number of things. Things he couldn't handle.

The first one was starkly real.

About fifty yards from the shore. A boat. And someone in the boat. And there was no mistaking who it was.

Jeremy Ketch.

Even from that distance, Giles could make out every line on Ketch's face, every hair in his dark beard. This was no shadowy ghost. Nothing pallid and wispy. He could see its eyes. Ketch's eyes.

And they were staring right at him.

Then the ghost began rowing toward the shore. Frightened, Giles had sought the refuge of the woods. And when he had gained a vantage point just below the old gold mine, he saw that the ghost of Ketch had disappeared. Dissolved.

Replaced by something much less substantial.

The shadow of a small child.

And somehow, he wasn't at all sure why or how, Giles knew it was the shadow of a little girl.

He knew . .

In absolute terror, he watched the shadow hover there over the darkening surface of the lake with the storm approaching. He thought perhaps he heard it call out something.

Perhaps his name . . .

"Officer Giles, we've got some banana cream pie tonight."

Startled, Giles twisted around to the voice of the young woman. The present reasserted itself. She was smiling apologetically.

"Officer Giles, did I scare you? I'm real, real sorry. You musta been thinkin' like fire about something."

"I . . . yeah, yeah, thinking about things. Peachface, did you mention something about pie?"

"Fresh banana cream. You like some?"

Her innocent smile gave him a rush of comfort.

"Sounds great on a rainy night. Yeah, give me a big sliver of it."

"It's really slammin' an' bangin' out there tonight, isn't it?"

The young woman slid a saucer overflowing with a piece of the pie in front of him.

"Looks pretty good," he said. "And, yeah, it's about a toad strangler rain."

Grinning, the young woman propped her elbows on the counter and said, "My granny used to say a hard rain brought out the hants."

"Hants? You mean, like ghosts?"

"Yes. Rain brings 'em out just like nobody's business."

Giles chuckled.

"But, Peachface, you don't believe in ghosts, do you?"

"I hadn't never seen one, but I don't go outta my way to find 'em neither. Whoops—got a customer. It's that Miss Boyle, the newspaper woman. Be back in a minute."

She swung away and Giles felt alone.

What deeply troubled him as he forked a couple of bites of the pie into his mouth was this: he didn't know what was going to happen next.

Things are movin' too damn fast.

Too damn fast.

He wondered whether seeing the ghosts *meant* something. Pondering such a metaphysical matter made his head do slow, stomach-turning loops. He put down his fork and pushed the saucer of pie away from him.

He gulped at his coffee, and his stomach shouted back at him.

Got to think what I'm gone do.

But he couldn't think. Couldn't concentrate.

It was the rain. The thunder. The lightning. And a little girl's voice.

"I'd lot rather work the day shift."

Giles blinked at the sudden reappearance of the young woman.

"Why's that, Peachface?"

"You won't tell nobody, will you?" She gestured for him to lean closer. Then she whispered, " 'Cause I'm scared of the dark."

Giles felt the beginnings of a smile toying with the corners of his mouth.

"Truth is," he said. "So am I."

"Oh, I bet you're not. I bet you're not scared of anything. Or anybody. But I am. I heard somebody talking when I came on my shift 'bout the Lightner girl. That scares me. They're saying somebody took her and's probably gonna kill her like what happened to that other girl. I bet you're not scared of who took her, are you?"

Giles swallowed.

"Maybe. Yeah, maybe some I am."

The young woman had an expression of mild surprise on her face.

"Oh, it's awful," she said. "Somebody taking her like that. Did you know she was in here just a few days ago? Sat right there on that stool."

Giles glanced at the spot two places from him where she was pointing.

"That right?"

"Yes. I got her a Coke. She ordered a Coke, and when I gave it to her she said someday she wanted to be a waitress. Now probably all she'll be is dead."

"Maybe, but—"

"How did it happen? Why'd somebody take her?"

Giles could feel something building in him. He braced his hands against the counter because he thought he might just explode.

"It was because she . . ."

The young woman waited.

"Because why?"

Suddenly Giles slammed a fist down on the counter.

"She wasn't being careful," he boomed.

Other customers looked up momentarily.

The young woman frowned.

"Oh . . . that's why?" she said.

Giles fumbled for some change for a tip. The coins jingled on the counter.

"There's somewhere I got to go," he said.

He was nearly out the door when the young woman said, mostly to herself, "Out'n a storm like this?"

Twenty-four

Clay waited in the old boat repair garage for the rain to let up. And while he waited, he rehearsed his apology. The problem was that the words wouldn't stay in place.

I'm sorry, Hillary, I was wrong to suggest . . .

Sentences refused to complete themselves. Because . . .

Because I don't really believe I'm wrong.

It felt dishonest to be planning to visit Hillary to apologize when he continued to believe that his imaging was on target. It had seemed to lead him to John Jaggery's.

Seemed?

He lifted the word in his thoughts to examine it as one might examine an unknown object.

Yes, "seemed."

Could he really be certain?

The patter of rain had softened.

But there was, however, one thing the long evening had made him aware of. One certainty.

I love Hillary Garrett.

Rushing in on the heels of that certainty, the possibility, of another: *it will never work between us*.

Pressed at that moment to explain precisely why, he would not have been able to offer anything convincing or reasonable.

Just a feeling.

It had something to do with the differences between them and how they "pretended" those differences did not exist or did not matter.

Horror had brought them together.

And death.

And it appeared, ironically, that the shadow of horror was threatening to dissolve their relationship entirely.

When the rain had slackened to a heavy mist, Clay pushed out in the skiff and, minutes later, tied up at the Garretts' dock. The house was virtually dark. Standing on their deck, he knocked at the back door. No one answered.

Could she be asleep?

No, it was much too early for her to be in bed.

Maybe she has a date—with that Tanner guy from the station.

"Damn it," he whispered. "Hillary, I'm sorry. I haven't told you that I really care for you, but I do."

Nice speech, dummy, but there's no one around to hear it.

He wasn't aware how long he stood on the Garretts' deck, wallowing in self-pity. Long enough at least for the mist to give him a chill.

It was on his way back down to the skiff that he thought of where else Hillary might have gone. And the thought fired a sudden panic in his chest. Each second burned.

He poled hard to John Jaggery's dock. Tied down. And felt the imaging press in at the corners of his consciousness. His head swam. He held onto a post to steady himself against a wave of dizziness.

A man and a little girl.

They came this way.

"But where did they go?" he whispered to himself.

Closer to Jaggery's house, the imaging lost some of its immediacy. Clay felt confused.

Where did they go?

John Jaggery, did you abduct Christina Lightner?

Have you murdered her?

An angry, frustrated, frightened part of him wanted to pound on Jaggery's door and demand answers to those questions. A more reasonable part insisted that he had no proof of Jaggery's involvement. Accosting the much respected man would be crazy.

For a few seconds, Clay studied the rear of the darkened house. There was another reason he had come—to see whether Hillary had come to visit her old friend.

As quietly as he could, Clay slipped through an unlocked screen door onto a porch area.

Hillary's been here.

But the sudden push of his imaging was inconclusive, a mixture of vague images, a collage of outlines suggesting that Hillary had been there a number of times.

When Clay ever so carefully peered in a window, he saw nothing. A lamp was on, but there was no sign of Hillary. No sign of anyone. Reluctantly, he turned away.

Someone was waiting for him on the dock.

"You have a good reason for bein' on this property, Mr. Brannon?"

Clay recognized the voice of Donnie Ray Giles several feet before the man's face, ambered by the beam of a flashlight he was holding, became visible.

"I was looking for someone."

"You wanna tell me who that someone is?"

Clay could hear the tension in the man's voice, could

see it in the way he stood there, rigid, unmoving, as if he were taking a stand against something.

"Not particularly."

"Mr. Brannon, it's my duty to inform you that you are officially under suspicion. So it'd just be a good idea if you'd tell me what you're up to."

It was then that Clay noticed the revolver on Giles's hip. He couldn't recall having seen Giles wear a gun before.

"Look, all I was doing was seeing if Hillary Garrett was at Jaggery's."

"Hillary Garrett? Why in the hell would she . . . ? Was she there? Has she been there?"

Clay shook his head.

"I guess not."

Giles appeared to relax his shoulders as if relieved.

"You best get on home. Keep yourself outta trouble."

"Are you expecting some kind of trouble?"

"Mr. Brannon, I'm just gone tell you this: stay the hell outta things tonight. Go on home. That'd be the best advice I could give you."

Twenty-five

The dark and silent room was filling up with voices.

This new one screamed and called out and beat upon the walls much more than the smaller voice did.

It was a good thing the dark and silent room, no longer silent, had compartments. You could keep the voices away.

But you could watch them.

The monitor flickered on.

First one compartment, then another.

You could keep an eye on them.

Your company.

Now you have them and you can do what you want with them.

Because your father said it was okay.

The smaller voice was like the one in the desert, the one you could hear just before the explosions and the light. And the burning.

A little girl's voice.

From the desert.

It could torture you.

There, in the desert, you couldn't get to it. It was like a mirage. It cried out. Then disappeared. But it kept haunting you. A spirit of the desert. Of misery. And pain.

Out there you couldn't get to it.

To strangle it.

Because that's what you needed to do.

* * *

Just that suddenly, Hillary made herself stop sobbing.
I've got to think.
My God, I've got to think.
Her palms and knuckles were bloody and raw and sore
from beating upon the walls; her throat was coated with
thorns from yelling and crying.

It was pitch black in the room.

A concrete floor and concrete walls.

She still could not fully comprehend what had occurred.
When Jaggery had flipped the switch for the bookcase to
slide out, revealing the dark closet, she thought she had
heard a voice. A little girl's voice. Like the one on the
phone.

At the door to the closet, Jaggery caught her arm and
whispered something: "I'm sorry, but you'll have to stay."
She had tried to pull away, and that's when someone else
came onto the scene. She sensed someone behind her, but
was unable to see a face. Strong arms swung around her,
one at her waist, one at her shoulder, a hand pressed across
her mouth with a rag.

And something which burned her nose and mouth and
eyes.

And she had fallen away from the light.

Whatever it was, it had put her out for only a few minutes. She had woken with a cold, nauseating realization:
Clay was right.

My God, John Jaggery. The man I admired and trusted.

She had called out his name again and again, for she
had continued to want to believe in him. Perhaps someone
was forcing him to help abduct her. There had to be an

explanation. But as her mind raced, one image ghosted past all the rest: the one of Jaggery and the girls' softball team.

I adored those little gals.

Wish I could have taken every one of them home with me . . .

Sitting on the floor, leaning her back against the wall, Hillary let the darkest thought of all seep into her consciousness: *I may be killed. I may never see Clay or anyone else again.*

When a television monitor high in one corner of the room flickered on, it startled her. Blue, gray, and black images flooded the darkness. Hillary blinked. She pushed herself to her feet.

And moved closer to the monitor.

The screen showed another concrete room, and in the center of it, half sitting, half lying on a blanket was a little girl—Christina Lightner.

Shadows claimed most of her face except for the eyes. Eyes which had experienced terror. And anticipated more.

"Oh, dear God," Hillary whispered.

She closed her eyes and felt her body tremble.

When she opened her eyes again and focused upon the monitor, the scene had shifted. The closed-circuit television monitor captured someone standing, arms folded.

Hillary stared at the image of herself.

And began to whimper like a frightened animal.

* * *

Hillary was still not home when Clay went to the Garretts' a second time. Neither were her parents.

She's out with Dave Tanner.

Damn it, I bet she is.

The strength of the wave of jealousy surprised him. But what struck him as ironic was that he actually *hoped* Hillary *was* with Tanner. Because that would mean that she wasn't at Jaggery's.

As he poled away from the Garretts' dock, Clay juggled a dark assortment of thoughts and fears. And questions.

What's going on with Giles?

How was it that he happened to be on Jaggery's dock?

Too many coincidences here.

Clay's imaging had suggested that Giles had something to do with the demise of Jeremy Ketch—what else was Giles involved with?

What the hell should I do now?

It seemed symbolically appropriate that he had poled back to the tie-down point under the cloak of darkness. In no respect had he reached a point of clarity—that is, except for one.

He knew he had to see Hillary.

Tonight.

Twenty-six

Clay was on his bike when another round of thunder-showers struck the lake area, forcing him to take shelter at the Marina Grill. The aroma of greasy hamburgers reminded him that he hadn't eaten since early afternoon—it was approaching midnight and his stomach was growling.

He sat at the counter and the young woman known as Peachface took his order of a hamburger, french fries, and a soft drink.

"Sure is some storm tonight," she offered. "Officer Giles calls it a toad strangler."

"Yeah," said Clay, "it was starting to rain too hard to be out on a bike." He was in no mood for small talk and hoped the young woman wouldn't press to continue the conversation.

"You got pretty wet," she said, eyeballing ringlets of his hair. "And I'm thinkin' Officer Giles is gettin' pretty wet if he's still out there somewheres."

A shadowy image of Giles stole into Clay's thoughts.
He's out there all right.
The question is: what's he up to?

Clay only nodded, and with that, the young woman gave her attention to the row of booths on the other side of the restaurant.

Breathing a sigh of relief, Clay pulled within himself.

He couldn't get Giles out of his thoughts; more precisely, he couldn't shake off what his intuition insisted upon: *Giles had something to do with the drowning of Ketch.*

No, he couldn't prove it.

And one thing more.

Giles knows something about the abduction of the Lightner girl.

But how deeply Giles was involved, Clay couldn't possibly determine. Not yet.

He thought again about John Jaggery. He thought again about the image of the man and the girl he had followed.

I'm missing something.

A piece of the puzzle.

After Peachface brought his food, he found he didn't have the appetite he anticipated. Two bites of the hamburger and a half-dozen fries were as much as he could stomach.

Hillary, where the hell are you?

The rain continued to fall. He was worried about her. He was angry with her. And most of all, he wanted to see her so that he could tell her something.

I love you.

He shook his head at the weird duality of his thinking. On the one hand, he was trying to solve the mysteries of the Foxpath Lake summer; on the other, he was coming to terms with his feelings about a young woman he'd only really known a few weeks.

Horror and love. Death and love.

Good stuff to write about.

But he never thought he'd be living the two at the same time.

"If you're not waiting for someone, would you like to

join me? I've got a booth in the corner. I'm hiding out there. How about it?"

Clay was pulled by Katie Boyle's voice, and he was held by her smile. At first he muttered, "No," but when she persisted, he shrugged and followed her to her booth.

She had three different notepads spread out on top of the table space. Stacking them neatly together, she smiled at him and said, "Great night for a murder mystery, huh?"

"Yeah, you could say that."

He was beginning to feel that he had made a mistake—that he should be on the Garretts' deck, waiting for Hillary to come home even if it meant getting soaked—when Boyle said, "You and I are both suspicious of Giles, aren't we?"

"Suspicious? How so?"

"Well . . . I think that both of us, for different reasons perhaps, wonder what really happened to Jeremy Ketch. Maybe a certain law enforcement official had good reason to want to see to it that Ketch drowned."

"But what do you mean by 'good reason?' Why would Giles want to kill Ketch?"

Boyle shook her head slowly.

Then she began to leaf through pages of one of the notebooks.

"I've done some research on Foxpath Lake—its history of drownings, to be more exact. Were you aware that Ketch had a little sister who apparently drowned here in the lake?"

Priddy Ann.

"No, I can't say that I was. But what's that got to do with Giles?"

"Well . . . it seems he was in the same boat with her when she . . . 'fell out.' Her body was never recovered."

"Doesn't sound like an ironclad case against him."

"No, but if Jeremy Ketch saw what really happened to his sister, he might one day have gained enough lucidity to say so. And our friend, Officer Giles, would have had a murder rap to deal with."

Clay rubbed at his temples.

"Listen, all of this boils down to a lot of speculation— that's about it. And, if you'll excuse me, there's someone I need to go see."

"Hillary Garrett?"

Clay had started to push away from the booth, but when he heard Hillary's name he stopped and smiled shyly.

"Perceptive. Very perceptive. But she and I are more interested in the Christina Lightner case than in the fate of Jeremy Ketch or Donnie Ray Giles. So I'll leave you on the trail of Giles. Good luck."

"I'm not on the trail of Giles—no. Donnie Ray Giles didn't abduct Christina Lightner, and he didn't kill Leigh Rybeck. But I think I know who might have. Giles probably knows, too. Stay a few more minutes and I'll explain. And then you can help me decide the next step to take."

Her invitation was too much to resist.

Clay sat down and listened.

From her large purse, Boyle retrieved a manila folder containing Xerox copies of confidential hospital records. Records from a nearby Veterans Administration hospital.

And from those documents Boyle spun a web of conjecture. Clay listened carefully.

And began to hear voices.

* * *

Sitting down again, leaning against the wall, Hillary calmed herself as best she could.

The TV monitor had winked off, leaving her in total darkness.

Although terrified, she clung to one reassuring thought: *Clay will come looking for me. I know he will. He'll come here.*

But would he come in time?

If John Jaggery were responsible for the death of Leigh Rybeck, wouldn't he kill again? He couldn't allow a captive to live.

"Please, Clay . . . I need you. My God, I need you."

The low crackle of sound startled her, for at first she thought it might be a rat. Instead, she discovered that the room had an intercom built high into one wall. There was more background crackle, and then a voice. The voice of John Jaggery.

"Hillary, I have no words to express how deeply sorry I am for what you're going through. Believe me, I share the horror. I share it intensely."

Her anger was like a lightning stroke. The fury of her words was generated from somewhere deep inside, from somewhere she'd never known, and that fury rushed into her throat and she stood and shouted toward the intercom.

"I hate you! I hate you! You bastard! You dirty bastard!"

And then, beginning to cry again, she slumped to the floor.

There was pity and sorrow in Jaggery's subdued tone.

"I deserve your hate, Hillary. I deserve whatever anger you feel. And I know that you will never forgive me . . .

I understand that. But you must listen to what I have to say in defense of myself and my actions. I can't provide you with a completely satisfying justification, and yet I know that you have a great capacity to assert your humanity—perhaps, even if you don't forgive, you will detect something very human in what I've done."

He paused. There was an audible click as he swallowed.

Hillary felt drained. Anger held the empty bowl of her emotions. She hated the sound of Jaggery's voice. She pressed her fingers over her ears to block out his explanation, though part of her wanted desperately to hear it, to understand what darkness had possessed the man whose friendship she had once valued above all others.

"The center of my life," he began, "would not hold after Velma died. I needed the bond of family. There was only Bill. Our Billy. After Desert Storm he had wandered around the country, trying to find himself. I wanted him to come back here. And he did. But he had changed. And he couldn't help himself."

The man paused again because his voice had begun to tear like tissue. He cleared his throat and continued.

"On the night of January 20, 1991, our Billy was deployed in Al Jubayl, about 200 miles south of Kuwait. He and a dozen or so other soldiers were on loan to a construction battalion. It was there, in the desert, that our Billy had started to hear voices—one in particular—the voice of a little girl, a voice carried along on the desert wind. Like some animal spirit of the desert. She was crying. Our Billy now thinks that the voice was a voice of warning."

Another pause. It seemed as if Jaggery were waiting

for some indication that Hillary was listening closely. He gathered himself again and continued.

"Something happened. An explosion. Fire. Lights. 'Mop level 4' was ordered—full chemical gear. Something happened. And not long after our Billy came home, he experienced physical problems: unexplained rashes and numbness. And he kept hearing the voice of that little girl, and it cut into him like a knife and so you see . . . he had to make it stop hurting him. No doctor could do it. He found his own way. And I . . . I helped. And Donnie Ray Giles, too. We built the shelter you're in. It's the only place our Billy can go where the war doesn't follow him."

Hillary breathed in the horror of the man's words as if his explanation were some poisonous vapor forced upon her. There was no way to turn off the intercom, nowhere to run from his words. She was trapped. And she knew that it was only a matter of time before Jaggery's "Billy" paid her a visit.

When Jaggery spoke again, it was almost as if he had read her mind.

"I don't think he'll hurt you, Hillary. It's just that he has no . . . control sometimes. There's a fire in his brain and only one way to put it out. And, you see, Billy's not our real son. He's adopted, and it's possible there's something hidden in his family history . . . or perhaps no other explanation is necessary beyond what happened in the desert that night a couple of years ago. Something happened. I'm sorry, Hillary. I can't stop him. I won't stop him because . . . I love him, love him too much to do what I would have to do. Velma loved him, too. We loved him as much as we would have loved a child we had created together. But you see, it's too late for me to stop him now. It's too late. I'm sorry. I'm very sorry."

His words cut off as if they had been recorded and the tape had run its course. Hillary cupped her elbows and rocked back and forth and silently prayed that Clay would come looking for her.

Immersed in her own misery, she had forgotten about Christina Lightner until she began to hear someone whispering in a far corner.

A little girl's voice?

"Who's there?" said Hillary.

And the whisper gained volume. Words became distinct.

"Help. Help me."

On her hands and knees, Hillary crawled toward the voice. Yes, a little girl's voice. And in the far corner she felt near where the floor met the wall, and her fingers made contact with a metal vent.

"Who's there?" Then the obvious possibility occurred to her. "Christina? Christina, is that you?"

"Yes. I'm Christina. Would you help me?"

"Oh, honey, I'll try. I'll try."

Hillary pressed her mouth closer to the vent and added, "Are you okay? Has anyone . . . hurt you? Are you okay?"

"I'm hungry. Who are *you?*"

"My name is Hillary Garrett, sweetheart. Listen, you'll be fine. Someone will be coming to find us, okay?"

"Are you in prison, too?"

Hillary hesitated.

Yes, that's exactly what it was.

"But we won't be much longer. Someone will be coming to get us out."

The little girl did not speak for several seconds. Then she said, "I don't think so. I don't think anyone's coming. Not even my grandpa."

"Oh, yes, honey. Yes. Yes, someone will come."

"I don't think anyone's coming. Why haven't they come? I want to go home. Help me. Please help me. Will you help me?"

"Yes . . . Christina. Yes, but we have to wait. Someone *will* come . . . I promise you. I promise."

And then she heard a noise which sent chills through her—the grating of concrete against concrete. Behind her somewhere, in the nearly palpable darkness, a door of some kind was opening. She heard a scuffle of movement. A flare of light.

Hillary held her breath.

And Christina Lightner screamed.

Twenty-seven

And when Boyle finished presenting her conjectures, she said, "What does it mean to you?"

But at first Clay did not respond. His thoughts had drifted back to the imaging of the man and the girl on Jaggery's dock. The man. Small. With small hands.

Where have I seen him before?

He shook free of his introspection and looked at Boyle.

"It means that Bill Jaggery could be dangerous," he said. "And it means there's somewhere I have to go. And I'm a damn fool and a coward for not being there already."

"Hey, take me with you," Boyle exclaimed.

But Clay was up and away from the booth and out the door before she could gather up her papers and purse. Out the door and into a soft rain. To Clay, it was a chilling rain. As chill as his thoughts.

"Your game's up. Now, damn it, you're going with me to Jaggery's, and you're going to call in whatever police help is needed. The Jaggerys have Christina Lightner, and I think they have Hillary, too. And you knew about this all along—damn you, you knew about it."

Clay pounded his fist on Giles's desk.

"Whoa, now, hold on. Let's . . . just calm yourself a mile or two, and let's talk ourselves through this."

"No. There's no time, and you know it. But you can stop it. You know the Jaggerys. You've been protecting them. Here's your chance to do the right thing, and if you won't, then I'm calling the police."

"And tellin' 'em what? Yeah, so you found out Billy Jaggery's got a kink in his brain—so what? Don't mean he kidnaps and kills little girls. And John Jaggery—one of the most respected men around. No one'll believe you, son. Not a soul. Because if you go over to the Jaggerys, I'll guarantee ya you won't find anything. Not a blessed thing."

Giles pitched back in his chair and lifted his boots onto his desk. He grinned a satisfied grin.

"You admit then that you know about the Jaggerys?"

"Friend, I'm not admittin' a damn thing. The investigation into the disappearance of that Lightner girl is underway. No leads at the moment."

"What about the death of Jeremy Ketch?"

Clay was pressing because suddenly many things were becoming clear. Pieces of the puzzle Boyle had placed before him. Yes, he thought he knew what Giles was covering up.

"Poor fella drowned. Case closed."

"You killed him," said Clay. "And tonight I understand why you did."

Giles's grin flickered.

"You don't know nothin'," he said.

"You killed Ketch because all the renewed attention to him this summer was a threat to you. Maybe because Ketch knew a dark little secret about you. About you and the death of his sister."

Giles laughed softly.

"You've been watchin' too many of them detective shows on TV, son. Ketch didn't even have a sister."

"Oh, yes, he did. Katie Boyle discovered he did. She also discovered that his sister drowned—allegedly drowned, that is."

Lowering his boots to the floor, Giles grunted. His sudden discomfort was visible.

"You're talkin' about old, old news. And you got no proof of nothin'. No witnesses. Nothin'."

"What about your little brother, Drew?"

The change in Giles's expression, the change in his tone and manner, was like watching some inevitable process, something natural, like the dying of the light at sunset.

"Damn it all to hell," he whispered. "You leave Drew outta this, y'hear me?"

"He was there, wasn't he? The day Ketch's sister drowned—your brother was there. He probably saw it all. If someone were to patiently ask him what happened, he—"

"Get outta here! Get the hell outta here!"

Giles's face was all fury and sadness. His voice quavered.

Clay backed away from the desk.

"I'm going," he said. "I'll be at Jaggery's. I won't call the police because I think you want to stop whatever's going on over there. You're the only one who can."

And with that, he turned and went out the door into the rain and the darkness.

Scrambling to the opposite side of the room, Hillary tried to make out a shape and movement where a new block of darkness had appeared. Her inclination was to stand up and take a run at the opening and at whoever was there.

Then, quite suddenly, a voice.

"Help me."

A little girl's voice.

But not the voice of Christina Lightner. She could still hear Christina who was now crying softly.

"Help me, please. There's a bad man who wants to kill me."

"Dear God," Hillary murmured.

It was the voice of the little girl who had been calling her. The same voice which had, weeks earlier, called 'Just Pretend.'

"Help me, please. It's almost time."

"It's okay," said Hillary. "It's okay. Someone will come."

An eerie silence followed.

Then, deep within the darkness a tiny light flared. It was like a candle. Hillary inched along the wall until she was nearly opposite the block of darkness, and yet it continued to be difficult to see much.

"I have a wish," said the little girl.

And Hillary felt drawn to the innocent hopefulness of the tone.

"Oh, honey . . . what's your wish?"

The darkness stirred.

The candlelight flickered and shuddered.

A small form, mostly buried by shadows, came into view. And Hillary experienced the sensation of hands reaching into her body and squeezing all of the air from her lungs.

The first line was spoken in a little girl's voice.

"Shiver and quiver, little tree."

But the second line was spoken in a man's voice.

"Silver and gold throw down over me."

Hillary pressed her hands against her lips.

A small man stepped forward so that he was almost completely visible. In a little girl's voice he said, "Don't you want to know who I am?"

Hillary cowered. Tears trickled down her cheeks. She could not speak.

The small man smiled a maniacal smile. Once again his voice was high and childlike.

"I'm not a little girl," he said. "I was only pretending. Like a game. Just pretend. I'll tell you who I really am." Then his voice deepened as he said, "I'm the bad man."

Twenty-eight

Clay pedaled as fast as he could through the light rain. He passed the Garretts' home, knowing there was no point in stopping to see whether Hillary was home. He was certain now that she was not.

I should have a gun or something.

I should have called the police.

Giles won't help.

I don't know what I'll be walking into.

But he knew there was no turning back. Hillary was in danger. Every ounce of his intuition told him so.

There was only one light on at Jaggery's house.

Carefully skirting the perimeter of the property, Clay pushed his bike to the rear of the house, leaned it against a tree and sneaked toward the back door. He had no specific plan—just to force his way in and demand the release of Hillary and of Christina Lightner, if she were being held there, too.

And if she's still alive.

At the back door, he closed his eyes and concentrated and, once again, experienced the image of Hillary.

She's here.

But when he touched the knob of the door, the blackness of the image he connected with was overwhelming.

He gasped. His knees buckled. He feared he would pass out.

He's come this way.

The bad man.

Taking quick, shallow breaths, Clay steadied himself and pushed at the door. And, to his surprise, it opened. His momentum carried him through one room and toward the muted light of the next.

"I've been expecting you."

A man's voice greeted him.

Details of the living room poured through Clay's senses, and then he focused on the man who was sitting in an easy chair in front of a television, the screen of which was filled with bright, gray-white snow.

The man remained seated but turned to face him.

He was pointing a large revolver at Clay's chest.

The man smiled weakly.

"Miserable night, isn't it?" he said. "And I assume you haven't come to pay a social visit. Am I correct?"

Gaining enough composure to speak, Clay said, "Let Hillary go. She's done nothing to you. Let her go. If you have to hold somebody as a hostage, hold me instead."

"Noble. Very noble. Oh, and you really needn't be afraid." He glanced at the revolver. "I've no plans to shoot you. This firearm belongs to Billy, my Billy. Marine issue. He had it with him in Desert Storm."

Clay drew himself up. There was defiance in his tone.

"I don't give a damn about the gun, and I'm not afraid of you or your son. Just let Hillary go."

Jaggery sighed.

"The situation here is rather complex. Oh, I could never explain it . . . here, I'll show you."

Jaggery switched something which resembled a televison remote control and the screen brought up the image of a little girl in a dark room.

"You'll see that no one's been hurt," Jaggery continued.

The screen flickered, and Clay's breath caught high in his chest. There was Hillary. She was on her hands and knees in the corner of a bare, darkened room.

Another flicker, and the face of William Henry Jaggery, black eyes bulging, appeared in a close-up. Aware that the camera was on him, the younger Jaggery smiled a maniacal smile.

The older Jaggery said, "My son. I built all of this for him. I thought it would help him . . . get back to normal. I thought I could help him put out the fire in his brain. But only one thing can, it seems."

He switched on an intercom mounted over the living room entrance and Hillary's voice wafted out from it. And Clay felt his heart swell as if it had been bruised violently. Hillary was talking softly with someone—Christina Lightner, Clay assumed. And then another voice intruded. A man's voice. Singing.

"Shiver and quiver . . ."

The lyric repeated over and over before suddenly ceasing. There were two loud beeps. John Jaggery stood up. He continued to train the revolver on Clay.

"What's going on?" Clay exclaimed.

"Wait a moment," said Jaggery. "Hillary's going to be released."

Clay was startled as the bookcase swung away to reveal a block of darkness. Then a grating noise, and Hillary was lifted up into the opening as if by an elevator. When she saw Clay she gave out a muted shriek and ran to his arms.

As Clay held her tightly, the voice of Billy Jaggery broke through static on the intercom.

"Father, these two are in my way. Take care of them so I won't have to. Father, you'll do that, won't you? For your son. Your loving son."

With Hillary pressed against him, Clay looked at John Jaggery. The man was shaking his head, though he had not lowered the revolver.

"No," he muttered, more to himself than to anyone else. "No, I can't cross that line. Not that one."

Seconds later, the dark opening from which Hillary had emerged was filled with Billy Jaggery; he was holding a forearm under the chin of Christina Lightner, pressing hard so that she couldn't scream.

His eyes were on his father. They flashed hatred and disgust.

"Hand it to me," he said, reaching toward the revolver. "This is not the season for cowards."

For an instant, it appeared that John Jaggery might aim the revolver at his son and pull the trigger, but then he glanced away and reluctantly relinquished the weapon.

Clay and Hillary could only watch, paralyzed by the horror of the moment.

Billy Jaggery tightened his hold on the little girl and then aimed the revolver at Clay's face.

"Shiver and quiver, my friend," he said.

"Drop it, Billy. And let go of the girl."

Clay and Hillary turned to see Donnie Ray Giles braced at the entrance to the living room, a two-hand grip on his revolver which was pointed at Billy.

But the younger Jaggery, momentarily surprised,

stepped back into the block of darkness, dragging the girl with him. He studied Giles for a score of heartbeats. He smiled.

"You hear the voices, too, don't you?" he said. "That makes you like a brother. No way in hell you're gonna shoot your brother."

"Please," said John Jaggery to Giles, "let him go. There's only one way he can be stopped now."

Giles lowered his gun.

Billy Jaggery and his captive dropped out sight.

Clay stepped toward Giles.

"You have to get him. Get him before he kills Christina."

John Jaggery moved between them and faced Giles.

"Don't do it. You don't know him. You don't know the darkness down there as well as he does."

Giles hesitated. He was trembling. He looked as if he'd seen a ghost.

"But I got to," he said. "It's the only thing I can do. I'll go down through the other entrance." He started to go, then hesitated again, and to Jaggery he said, "I do know 'bout the darkness. I know it the same as Billy does."

And then he was gone.

The seconds ticked away.

"I'm calling the police," said Clay.

But before he could reach the phone, a single shot rang out. And the silence which followed would live with Clay and Hillary for years to come.

"Oh, Christina, my God," Hillary cried.

Clay held her and looked at Jaggery.

"Did he get him?"

Jaggery shook his head.

"No. No, Giles would never be able to. My Billy . . . he's put out the fire in his brain the only way possible."

Twenty-nine

The end of summer.

Hillary knew what the silence meant.

And yet, it was deceptive. The silence. And then, of course, the beauty of Foxpath Lake seen from the deck of her parents' house at sunset. It was also deceptive.

The lake had hidden horror.

But now it was time to move on. Time to move past the silence. What had her mother said?

But when you hear only silence, then you'll know we've stopped trying.

Charmian approached with a pitcher of lemonade, and Hillary had to smile because she knew that when Charmian was troubled these days and did not know what else to do, she made a pitcher of lemonade.

"You be missin' this house, woncha now?"

Hillary nodded.

"Yes. I'll miss it especially at this time of day. The color of the sky. The serenity. It's difficult to believe that so many terrible things could have taken place this summer here, near such a beautiful lake."

"I know that's right. An' you be fine in town? You and your mama?"

"The Fox Hollow apartments—they're nice. Not far

from school. Mom'll be back from the treatment center next week, and then we'll move. Dad said he'd help. I'm not sure where he'll be living—back here for awhile, I guess. Until he can sell the property."

"I be real sorry 'bout your folks, they didn't make it together. Real sorry."

"Thanks, Charmian, I know you are." She reached out for the woman's hand and squeezed it. "They tried. I think they tried as hard as they could. Mom's health is the thing I'm most concerned about now. She'll be starting a new life when she returns from the center."

"I be prayin' for her."

"I know you will."

"An' . . . I be missin' you. Missin' doin' for you."

"Oh, Charmian, I'll miss you, too. But you've already promised you'll visit Mom and me as often as possible."

She saw tears in the woman's eyes; she stood up and hugged her. And the embrace ushered in a silence, the best kind of silence.

They parted when the silence was broken by the sound of footsteps coming up onto the deck.

"It's your friend, I'm supposin'."

"Yes," said Hillary, and she watched as Charmian hurried away.

Then she turned and Clay was there, his hand raised in a gesture of greeting, and he said, "Hi . . . I was hoping I'd find you here."

"One of my favorite spots," she said. "I'm going to miss it."

There was another silence.

And Hillary knew the meaning of this one, as well. The love they felt for each other couldn't change that meaning.

"Charmian has some lemonade," she followed. "Have a glass."

Clay smiled shyly.

"Sure."

A few moments later they were standing at the railing of the deck, the sky painting the lake a gold that could never be reproduced.

"The media seems to be losing interest in Foxpath Lake finally. Moving on to other sordid stories, I guess."

Clay agreed.

"I'll just be glad when all the hearings and court stuff are over. Telling the same story again and again has gotten old. I hear they're still not certain what kind of charges to bring against Giles and John Jaggery. I wish I could have—"

"No, Clay. You did what you could have. What can anyone do about someone like Bill Jaggery? His father should have stopped him—I know some will say that—but he couldn't bring himself to do it. I'm not defending him. I just feel so deeply sorry for him. And, in a way, Giles, too."

"I feel sorry for Christina Lightner. She kinda reminded me of Molly. Will she ever be able to put the memories of this behind her?"

Hillary shook her head.

"Remember Molly's dream?" she said. "About the dark box and you and I trying to save someone? It was amazingly close to what happened."

"Yeah," said Clay.

And Hillary could tell that there was something else on his mind. Not dreams. Or the horror of the summer.

She found herself clutching at the pendant around her

neck. The one Molly had given her. The broken heart pendant.

"Clay . . . go ahead and say what you've come to say."

He tried but couldn't look into her eyes. His words seemed to be directed at the lake.

"My mother's going to Louisiana. To be closer to my father. I think it's a mistake, but . . . I can't let her go alone. So, you see . . . I'll be leaving in the morning."

"But you'll be coming back, won't you?"

Her heart was beating so rapidly she feared he would hear it.

"I don't know. I'll probably go my senior year out there, and then . . . I'll see how things are going."

Hillary sighed. She felt silly doing so. She wanted to handle this as maturely as possible. She had sensed that it was coming.

"I have something for you—a going away gift," she said.

When she returned from the house, she handed him a small, spiral notebook.

"A new writing journal."

He took it, and for a moment couldn't speak.

"Thanks. Thanks . . . this means a lot. And, well, the one Molly gave me is pretty full, so I was needing a new one. I'm sorry I didn't bring anything for you."

"You've given me enough."

"Hillary, I wish we could just pretend—" He stopped mid-sentence and rolled his eyes. "Oh, sorry, poor choice of words."

"We can," she said. "We have one more evening together. Stay as long as you can."

"I will," he said.

They stood together at the railing.

They listened to the silence of the lake.

Until it, too, was broken.

A cry? Or was it singing? A nursery rhyme? A child's lyric?

A little girl's voice.

About the Author

J.V. Lewton lives with his family in Auburn, Alabama. He is currently working on his next young adult horror novel. J.V. loves to hear from his readers and you may write to him c/o Zebra Books. Please include a self-addressed stamped envelope if you wish a response.

*Please turn the attached page for
an exciting sneak preview of*

The Crush II
by
Jo Gibson

Prologue

Judy Lampert had never been so mad in her life. Her face was red, her heart was pounding, and she felt like screaming in pure frustration as she knelt down on her adoptive parents' immaculately kept lawn and peered through a gap in the hedge. There was a party going on next door. She'd seen her friends pull into the driveway and get out of the car, carrying platters of food. But she hadn't been invited!

It was August in southern California, and the afternoons were bright and sunny. The broiling heat of July had passed, and it was no longer necessary to run the air conditioning twenty-four hours a day. It was perfect weather for a party, and that seemed to be what was happening next door. Cars had been arriving for the past thirty minutes, pulling into Mr. and Mrs. Warden's driveway and parking in front of the house.

Judy had been in her bedroom suite when she'd heard music coming from the patio next door. It wasn't the type of music that Michael's parents would enjoy. This was rock music, excellent rock with a driving beat that made Judy's feet tap and wiggle with the desire to dance. But why were Michael's parents hosting a teenage party when their only son, Michael, was locked away at Brookhaven Sanitarium? It just didn't make sense.

The gardener had just watered the lawn, and Judy felt moisture seep through the knees of her jeans. That didn't matter. She had several new pairs hanging in her closet, and she had plenty of time to change clothes before she went to her night job at Covers, the teenage nightclub in Burbank. Getting her clothes wet didn't bother Judy in the least. Her primary concern was finding out exactly what was happening next door.

Judy parted the scratchy branches of the boxwood hedge so she could see most of the patio. Her drama teacher at Burbank High was sitting on a tall director's chair, surrounded by several people from Covers. Mr. Calloway owned Covers, and most of his staff were students. As Judy watched, Linda O'Keefe, one of the singers at Covers, grabbed Mr. Calloway's hand and pulled him up to dance with her. Linda had sung several duets with Michael before all the trouble had started.

As Judy watched, Andy Miller, the short order cook at Covers, whirled into view. Andy was dancing with Carla Fields, and they looked so funny, Judy almost giggled out loud. With his carrot-red hair and the extra inches around his waist, Andy wasn't any girl's dream guy. But he could certainly do better than Carla!

Carla was the assistant manager at Covers, a nice girl but not the type that any boy would look at twice. Carla had nondescript brown hair pulled up into a bun, and she wore horn-rimmed glasses. Today she was dressed in her usual outfit, a baggy skirt and an over-sized blouse. Carla came from a poor family, and her clothes were all thrift store bargains. She didn't own anything that fit her properly.

Judy watched for a moment, and then she shrugged. Carla and Andy looked as if they were having fun. Perhaps it was a good match, after all. They were both born losers, and no one else would even think of dating them.

Alberto Cordoza, one of the waiters at Covers, came out of the house, carrying a platter of snacks. Judy had gone out with Berto while Michael was dating his sister, Nita. Berto hadn't approved of Nita's romance with Michael, and neither had Judy. She'd wanted Michael for herself. But then Nita had become the fifth victim of the "Cupid Killer," the name the police had given to the serial killer who'd left arrows at the scene of the murders, thrust into the dead victims' chests.

Since all the murdered girls had dated Michael, he was the prime suspect. But the police couldn't arrest him now, not while he was at Brookhaven Sanitarium for psychiatric evaluation.

Judy's eyes were drawn to the red and white banner that was strung over the patio. It said "WELCOME HOME" in big block letters. Could this mean that Michael had been released? No, that was impossible. Surely someone would have told her. The banner must be for someone else. But who?

Just then, Judy spotted Vera Rozhinski, the bartender at Covers, mixing her special nonalcoholic fruit drinks behind the patio bar. Vera's parents had sent her off to visit her grandmother in New Mexico, right after the Cupid Killer had struck for the fourth time. Of course, Vera hadn't been in any danger. She'd never dated Michael, and she hadn't been serious about the contest the other girls had started.

Judy frowned as she thought about the contest and how much grief it had caused. Michael had just broken up with Liz Applegate, his girlfriend at U.C.L.A., and the contest had started as an effort to cheer him up. All the Covers' girls, with the exception of Judy and Carla, had decided to make a play for Michael. The object had been to date him for two solid weeks, and Deana Burroughs, a singer at Covers, had almost won. But the Cupid Killer had murdered her the night before she could be declared the winner.

That should have been enough to warn the other girls away, but no one had believed that Deana had been murderd just because she'd been dating Michael. Judy had tried to convince them that the contest was dangerous, but no one had listened. They'd all assumed it was a random killing, until it had happened again.

Becky Fischer, the club comedienne, had picked right up where Deana had left off. She'd dated Michael for over a week before she'd been killed. Mary Beth Roberts, their featured dancer, had been the third victim. And that was when everyone at Covers had started to panic.

Judy had told everyone her theory, that the arrows the killer left behind were a warning about the dangers of love. But no one had paid any attention to her. Despite Judy's warning, Ingrid Sunquist, a waitress at Covers, had dated Michael next, and she had been the next victim. Finally, Nita had fallen prey to the Cupid Killer.

Over a month had passed since the last murder. The police still suspected Michael. It was true that there had been no more killings while he'd been behind locked bars, but that didn't prove that he was the killer.

Judy had gone out to Brookhaven every week, even though Michael's doctor wouldn't let her in to visit. It was a terrible misunderstanding, and she needed to talk to Michael to straighten it out. She'd signed the complaint that had sent him to Brookhaven, but she'd only done it to save him. The police had been ready to arrest him, and Judy had known that he wasn't the Cupid Killer.

She'd thought the whole thing out very carefully. Michael had no alibis for the times of the murders, and he might have been convicted if he'd gone to trial. Since California had the death penalty, Michael might have even been executed. Judy had saved his life by signing that complaint, and once she'd expalined it, she was sure that Michael would agree. Sitting behind locked doors at Brookhaven was a lot better than pacing the floor on Death Row!

Judy drew in her breath sharply, as she caught sight of Michael's parents. Mrs. Warden was much thinner, and her hair was almost completely gray. Mr. Warden hadn't changed all that much, but Judy knew he was probably suffering just as much as his wife. It must be terrible to have a son accused of murder, a son who was locked up in a mental institution.

As Judy watched, Vera smiled at Michael's mother and handed her a drink. And Mrs. Warden put her arm around Vera's shoulder. So this was a welcome home party for *Vera*. But why were Michael's parents hosting the party?

Judy reached out and pushed the rest of the branches aside. Now she had a full view of the patio. Someone was sitting on a stool by the doorway, and she gave a little cry of surprise as he turned her way. It was Michael! Michael was out, and no one had told her! She had a right to be at his welcome home party. After all, she had saved his life.

It was agony to watch all her friends having fun, and to know that Michael was with them. Judy knelt on the damp ground for what seemed like hours, feeling terribly sorry for herself.

At last, the party began to break up, and Judy watched as the guests left, one by one. Now it was just the Warden family, and Judy leaned closer so she could listen. Michael's parents didn't say anything important, just how glad they were to have Michael home. Judy was almost ready to go back to her house, when she heard something that made her heart race in her chest. Michael's parents were talking about a dinner invitation. If they left Michael alone, she'd have a chance to talk to him!

"Are you sure you don't want to join us for dinner?" Mrs. Warden reached out to take Michael's hand. "The Jacobsons invited you, too."

"No, thanks. And don't worry about me. I'm going to take a drive up Laurel Canyon and spend some time at the lookout. I promised Dr. Tunney I'd start working on my music again, and I'd like to have one song finished before I go back."

"Well . . . all right." Michael's mother looked disappointed, but she smiled, anyway. "Whatever you think is best, dear."

Michael glanced at his watch. "Hey, it's almost six-thirty. Don't you have to be there at seven?"

"You're right." Michael's father stood up. "We'll see you when we get back, son. And if you need us, just call."

"Are you going to stop at Covers for the show?" Michael's mother looked concerned.

"No, Mom. Dr. Tunney doesn't think I'm quite ready for that. He doesn't want me to run into . . . well, you know who. I talked to Mr. Calloway, and I told him I want to peform again. But he understands why I can't do that right now."

Judy's hands were trembling as she released her hold

on the branches. Now she knew why she hadn't been invited to the party. It was the same reason Michael wouldn't be going to Covers to see the show. Michael didn't want to run into her!

It was terribly unfair, and there were tears in Judy's eyes as she walked back to the house and dressed in clean jeans. She could see the driveway from her window, and she watched as Michael's parents got into their car and drove off. There was only one thing to do. It would take courage, but she'd never been afraid of a challenge. Now that Michael was alone, she'd march right over there and confront him directly.

Judy squared her shoulders and hurried down the stairs. She walked resolutely across the lawn again and stepped through the gap in the hedge.

"Hi, Michael." Judy put on her best smile, but Michael didn't look very happy to see her.

"Judy." There was a frown on Michael's handsome face. "What are *you* doing here?"

Judy's smile wavered, but she managed to keep it in place. "I came to say welcome home. And I understand why you didn't invite me to your party. You don't realize that I saved your life."

"You what!?"

There was a shocked expression on Michael's face, but Judy ignored it as she rushed over to hug him. "I'll explain it all in a minute. But first I want to know about you. How long will you be home?"

"I'm on a weekend pass." Michael stepped back, out of her embrace. "And I was about to leave. I have to . . . uh . . . be somewhere in less than an hour."

Judy knew that waas a lie, but she didn't let on that

she'd eavesdropped on Michael's conversation with his parents. She just smiled and moved toward Michael again. "That's okay. This won't take long, and I have to leave soon, too. The show starts at eight, and I have to set up, for the new singer."

Michael looked very uncomfortable, and he took another step back. "Sorry, Judy. I really don't have time to talk."

"I just wanted to explain why I signed that complaint to get you locked up at Brookhaven. You see, I knew the police were going to arrest you for the murders, and it was the only way I could keep them from doing it. You're safe at Brookhaven, Michael. They can't put you on trial if the doctors say you're crazy. Now you can understand why I had to do it, can't you?"

"Judy . . . I . . . I really have to leave now."

Michael took a stsep toward the house. Judy managed to cut him off by grabbing his arm, but it was clear he didn't want to be close to her. "Come on, Michael. I only did what was best for you, and you ought to be grateful. And I'm so glad to see you again! How about a kiss for old time's sake?"

Michael gave a bitter laugh. "What old time are you talking about? The last time I saw you, you told Detective Davis that I tried to kill you!"

"Please, Michael. I already explained why I had to do that." Judy got a good grip on his arm and pulled him closer. "Let's be friends again. It used to be so nice."

"You're deluding yourself, Judy. It was never nice. The past few weeks have been a nightmare!"

"I know." Judy slipepd her other arm around Michael's shoulders and hugged him tightly. "I'm really sorry about that, but everything's okay now. Don't you see, Michael?

If you have to go to trial, you can get off by claiming temporary insanity."

"I'm not the one who's insane. *You* are! *You* killed them all. Not me!"

Judy shuddered at the cold expression in Michael's eyes, but she took a deep breath and went on. "I'll wait for you, Michael. I promise. And then we can pick up the pieces and start over. I know we can!"

Michael tried to break away, but Judy just hugged him tighter. She rubbed her breasts up against his chest and snuggled her body against his. "I don't care what people say, Michael. I'll always love you. Forever and ever. Don't you believe me?"

"Oh, I believe you!" Michael stared down at her, his eyes as cold as glaciers. "Listen to me, Judy. I don't want your love. I never did, and I never will. All I want is for you to leave me completely alone!"

"You don't really mean that." Judy wrapped her arms around Michael's neck and forced his lips down to hers. A kiss would do it. There was no way Michael could resist her kisses. But Michael's lips were like granite, cold and firm with no hint of passion. Even though Judy tried to make him respond, kissing Michael was like kissing a stone statue.

And then Michael thrust her back so hard, she almost fell. Judy stumbled and looked up at him, tears in her eyes. "I . . . I don't understand! You used to like to kiss me! We were such good friends!"

Michael turned on his heel and walked toward his house. He opened the door, and then he turned back to look at her. "Forget it, Judy. Crawl back in the same hole you crawled out of, and don't bother me again. I'll never forgive you for what you did to me!"

Judy gave a deep sigh of resignation as he strode into the house and slammed the patio door behind him. It wouldn't do any good to pound on the door. Michael wouldn't let her in. He was still so angry about being locked up in Brookhaven, he wasn't thinking straight.

There was nothing to do but go home. Judy stepped back through the gap in the hedge and hurried into her house. When she got to the privacy of her bedroom, she sat down on the bed and stared at her reflection in the mirror. She was prettier than any of Michael's dead girlfriends. With her light blond hair, deep green eyes, and perfect figure she could attract any other boy she wanted. But Judy wanted Michael. He was the only one who could make her truly happy. And Michael had rejected her. Again.

Tears rolled down Judy's cheeks, and she didn't even bother to blink them back. She couldn't really blame Michael for being upset. He was still a suspect in the murders, and he'd never forgive her for that.

Judy's mind spun in crazy circles. There just had to be some way to get Michael to forgive her. Life wasn't worth living without his love. She had to prove to Michael that she loved him more than life itself.

The moment Judy thought of it, she raced to the desk for a pen and some paper. There was only one way to make Michael forgive her. It was drastic, but she would do it. Michael had loved her before. Judy was sure of it. And after tonight, he'd love her again, throuighout eternity.